The House by the Lake

The House by the Lake

Adriana K. Wood

The House by the Lake
and other stories

The House by the Lake and other stories
ISBN 978 1 76109 463 7
Copyright © text Adriana K. Wood 2023
Cover image: Adriana K. Wood

First published 2023 by
GINNINDERRA PRESS
PO Box 3461 Port Adelaide 5015
www.ginninderrapress.com.au

Contents

The House by the Lake

A small dark blue car sped along the winding coastal road. A glittering expanse of lake that shimmered like a portal in a science fiction movie spanned the horizon on one side. It hit her peripheral vision in a mesmerising way. She gripped the wheel and tried to focus on the road ahead. On the other side, there were rolling fields dotted with clumps of trees, the grass coarse and yellow. White sheep dotted the pastures. Farmhouses were well out of sight, generally down long gravel drives.

Jacky doggedly continued driving along the narrow and gravelly road. In places, water gushed over the road from streams. She wondered what welcome, if any, she would get at the old homestead. They might well just turn her away, even if she were kin, as she had been away so long. Her mother, Lillian, had been tall and slender, while she was too short to look willowy. She resembled her mother, though, and had long reddish, brown hair falling around her shoulders, fair skin and blue eyes. She wondered if they would remember her there. She had been named Jacky by her father, after a pioneering ancestor whose first name was Jack.

Suddenly, she could see the homestead up ahead. There were black rocks and crashing waves towards the far side. The black rocks were part of a jagged headland. Fierce waves were hurled over the rocks, streaking them with white foam that crawled backwards to join the next oncoming wave. She had heard stories of a Japanese ship washed up against these rocks during the wartime era. Her Scottish ancestors had escaped from the land clearances in the Highlands where landlords were creating huge farms by evicting the traditional tenant farmers. The highlanders were driven to immigrate to what were once colonies like New Zealand. It seemed to her that her paternal ancestors had built a homestead in the most wild, remote place where any rapacious pursuers would be hurled over the cliff and down to the ferocious seas and rocks like jagged teeth below.

Jacky parked the rental car. She walked up the gravel driveway. The closer she got, the more she could see the house was dilapidated now with brown timber showing through white paint. A few Border collies, looking a bit unkempt, enthusiastically ran to greet her, acting as if they were bored and were desperate for human company.

Jacky knocked on the door. After a pause, she heard heavy foot steps approaching the door.

A man with wild black hair and sloppy clothes thrust his head out of the door. 'What do you want?' he asked in a surly way.

Jacky remembered Lachlan. She saw his childish features and wiry body somewhere within this now stocky, sullen man.

'Hello, Jacky,' he said in surprise. 'You don't look much different. You're still short like a child.'

'Well, you are very much taller,' she replied, not sure how to take his rather curt response.

He held the door open, gesturing for her to enter a long, dark passageway. She walked into a dark hallway that disappeared into shadows through the dark cavernous house. A shabby lounge room, with a TV blaring football, led off the corridor.

'Why are you here?' Lachlan demanded. He wasn't very welcoming but often men weren't welcoming by nature.

Jacky had planned to declare she wanted answers now about her ancestors and about all the gloomy secrets and relations when she and her mother had lived here after her father died. She had been ten to fourteen then. Now she was twenty-five. It seemed to her that her words would echo meaninglessly down the dark passage and disappear.

'I was homesick,' she joked, grinning.

Lachlan's pale gloomy face looked stunned before breaking into a grin.

A white-haired woman, Janet, with bent shoulders, came softly down the hall. Jacky remembered her when she had auburn hair and broad shoulders. She was very much paler and smaller now. Jacky had been a bit frightened of her once.

'Oh,' she said, startled upon seeing Jacky, who she seemed to dimly remember.

Jacky suddenly decided she would stay at the old hotel further back down the road. The hotel looked shabby but now seemed very bright compared with the old homestead.

'I wanted to ask about my father's family,' Jacky explained.

'Didn't he tell you anything?' asked Janet curtly.

'Well, he died when I was only ten,' Jacky reminded Janet.

'You should remember what he said,' Janet said, rather grumpily.

Jacky had come here with her mother, Lillian, after her father had died when they had got too far behind in their rent. They had lived here for about four years. Her mother had always softly murmured about how they would be going back to England soon but they never did, until all of a sudden, when Jacky was fourteen, they had left for England rather abruptly. Lately, questions about this house, its occupants and history, had haunted her. She didn't know why the house had so much power over her, almost like a living presence.

'How long will you be staying?' Janet asked frostily.

'I'll go stay at the old hotel,' Jacky replied.

'That place,' declared Janet. It was like a battle challenge to Janet if Jacky stayed at that Devil's den, as she saw it, and so she abruptly ordered Jacky that she must stay. She would show her a room.

'I'll come back later,' Jacky said. 'I want to go outside and explore first.'

Janet looked put out. 'I'll see you later,' she said disapprovingly.

Jacky found the faded yellow tussocky path that led to the shining lake far below. A coach full of tourists was parking in the gravel car park in front of the hotel. She walked carefully down to the lake. The sun glared off the lake into her eyes. Pebbles scrunched under her feet. Unlike the sea, there were ripples over the lake as if it were being shaken.

There were scrubby bushes around the edges. She vaguely remembered picnics on the shore and walking around the lake throwing pebbles into the water as there was nothing else to do. The shining, moving surface always had a hypnotic quality that drew her to linger by the shore. The vegetation was faded brown, almost sepia, and bleached yellow in places, pale green showing through. The surrounding area was very nondescript but the lake enveloped her senses as it danced and shimmered as if it had a life all of its own. She felt immersed in its sparkling depths.

She climbed back up the tussocky path to enter the hotel. She sat down in a corner, facing the window. The sparkling, silver-tinted lake looked as hypnotic and beautiful from the window and was shining dazzling white in places and seemed to beckon her into its mysterious depths.

'Hello,' a voice softly spoke.

She started and looked around to see a woman smiling hesitantly at her.

'I'm Jenny,' she told Jacky hesitantly. 'Leila, the Maori lady in charge of the café section, told me you were here. You are Jacky, aren't you?'

The woman was average height with longish, square-cut, blonde hair. Her eyes, like half moons, were blue.

'I was with your husband Ryan before you,' Jenny said. 'We had a son, Asher. I went by Libby then, short for Liberty-Jane, but I've settled for plain old Jenny now after so much has happened beyond my control. I can't fight it any more.'

Jacky remarked, 'Ryan had wives and women all over the place. I expect I'll run into a few of them. I think Asher is his only child. The last I heard he'd changed his name to Ryan and renamed Asher Adam.'

Jacky turned around to see a blond teenage boy who looked very like his mother but with untidy longish hair.

Ryan had as if softly unpeeled her heart and thrown it away mostly uneaten. She felt distanced from him now as if she had floated away from him, a bit like the Pink Floyd song 'Comfortably Numb', although she didn't do drugs.

'May I join you?' Jenny quietly asked. She sat down facing Jacky over the table but in a quiet, non aggressive way. 'Ryan lived with me for years near the township. One day he took off with Asher. They ended up in Germany. Asher eventually came home of his own accord. He's very resourceful and bright but seems so lost somehow.'

Jenny looked as if she was deliberating over telling Jacky something. She looked nervously away, out the window. 'I don't think Asher was Ryan's son now,' she said quietly.

'You mean a love triangle?' asked Jacky.

'There's no real love in Ryan,' Jenny said. 'He's quite destructive in his quiet, focused way.'

'I agree,' Jacky replied. 'What you really mean to tell me is you prefer to think Ryan is not Asher's father now. Love can end up that way.'

Jenny smiled, her icy eyes warming up.

Asher came over to the table.

'I suppose you want money for a drink,' Jenny said to him. 'Go to the café section and get a Coke. You're underage for the pub.' She handed over some money.

'He looks nothing like Ryan,' Jacky said. 'He looks as if he's been cloned off you.'

Jenny suddenly looked very nervous. 'I'd better go,' she said.

She and Asher walked out of the building.

Leila came over to talk to Jacky. Leila was a friendly, well dressed Maori woman with a typically sturdy and capable build. 'I suppose Jenny told you all about her marriage,' she remarked.

Jacky replied, 'It doesn't concern me.'

'It's really weird,' Leila replied.

'Love mostly is,' Jacky replied. 'Break-ups can make people go weird for a time. And gossip soon gets everywhere even if everyone says to not tell anyone else.'

Leila went back behind the counter, clattering about with things. Kitchens always echoed so much it was more peaceful to have coffee at home. Jacky walked outside and got in her car to drive into town.

The town was a picturesque tourist town now with cafés and restaurants and bright shops appealing to tourists. Jacky recognised an old schoolmate, Sheryl.

'The older locals won't work in town now and don't like the outsiders and tourists coming here,' Sheryl said. 'I didn't know you'd come home.'

'I haven't. I'll be leaving soon,' Jacky replied.

'Well, I must get going,' Sheryl said abruptly, hurrying off. She had reclassified Jacky as one of those strangers in town, especially as Jacky had a more English accent now which set her apart as soon as she spoke.

Jacky found it hard to believe they had always sat side by side in most classes and chattered all the time. Sometimes those with whom you had talked with the most ended up the least of your friends when push came to shove. She would be leaving soon anyway.

Jenny had parked nearby. She was with Asher.

'Hello,' she greeted Jacky, smiling. She had a rather strange, enigmatic smile. At least she was friendly.

Jacky noticed a sticker of Buddha on her rear window with a text 'MAY ALL BEINGS BE SAFE AND HAPPY.'.

Jenny pointed out a café. 'Let's go in there,' she said, 'and we can talk.'

Her warmth melted the cold feeling Jacky was beginning to feel again ever since she had come back, as if this town had put an emotionally freezing spell on her. It wasn't black magic but just human indifference in a small town or wherever you found it.

Jenny and Asher were already going into the café. Jacky followed and they sat down at a table. Jacky felt that whatever outlandish thing Jenny told her, at least it was good to sit down over coffee and talk with a friendly person.

'Asher is bullied a lot,' Jenny said sadly.

'They think I'm part alien,' Asher said with a youthful lack of reticence.

Jenny tried to shush him.

'You are alien and proud of it,' Jacky said cheerfully, thinking it must be a case of too much science fiction.

'Yes. That's it,' Asher grinned.

'He's being home-schooled after bullies broke his ribs,' Jenny said flatly.

'Did you get the police involved?' asked Jacky, horrified.

'I did want to call police but Asher didn't want them involved,' Jenny replied. 'I don't trust odd people who turn up at the local school especially wanting to test him and a few of the local kids too just to make it look as if they're not just interested in him.'

Jacky thought she must be imagining things about experts visiting schools just to test Asher but she remembered a few of those visiting counsellors and assessors could be very inappropriately nosy and arrogant. As a schoolgirl, she had never trusted them as they obviously thought it safe to bully school children in out of the way country areas. A woman counsellor had tried to shove her physically around, which was very bizarre. Jacky had run away.

The Maori waitress brought out a pot of herbal tea for two with tea cups and slices of gluten- free loaf. Asher had got a can of Coca Cola.

'He picked up that in Germany,' Jenny remarked, 'Coca Cola and hamburgers and junk food. He's just young and I can't change his tastes now. He'd probably run away if I tried to change him.'

'Like I ran away from Ryan,' Asher replied.

Jenny said to him, 'I'm just glad you're back.'

'Jacky could stay with us, Mum,' Asher said. 'We've heaps of room.'

'We're much closer to town,' Asher said to Jacky.

Jacky didn't want to be closer to this small, unfriendly town. She would be going soon anyway.

In a section of the café were displays of shimmering New Zealand Paua jewellery, in rippling, greens, pinks and blues and mauve. As a little girl, she had picked up whole shells off the sand, with their rough white backs and inner jewelled colours. It was a highly commercial business now linked with the tourist trade and thirst for souvenirs. There were no shells like that lying on the beach any more.

Later, Jacky found a Paua pendant in her bag. Asher must have put it there. It would be too awkward for both herself and Asher to return the pendant. In the end, she returned to the café and put some notes into the tips jar covering the cost of the pendant.

She walked around the town. She saw a few local people about who looked vaguely familiar but no one spoke to her. Nevertheless, she knew word would spread around that she was back, that girl who took off with her stuck-up English mother who thought they were better than them. She ended up driving back to the old homestead.

The front door still wasn't locked, like in the old days. She went to her room and took out her tablet. She checked her emails.,

Hi, Cindy,

What are you doing? Are you still in Spain? I'm in my long ago home town in the old homestead which is very rickety now and it looks like a haunted house.

I've met a strange teenager in town who says kids at school think he is part alien. He somehow moved a Paua shell pendant into my bag without me noticing. I gave the Waitress a huge tip to pay for it as anything else would make trouble for him or most probably for me seeing I'm the outsider here. The locals are a bit cold except for a friendly Maori woman. They probably remember me as the girl who left town with her stuck up English mother. The old homestead is virtually empty now except for Janet who is old and white haired now and Lachlan who is scruffy. He's a few years older than me. He's been around but he is back there now.

Write soon.

Jacky

An email quickly came back.

Hi, Jacky,

Good to hear from you. Don't worry about those locals. That teenage boy sounds like a type with power like Uri Geller. Tell him he needs to get a job and you won't see him for dust. He is like a stage magician. They divert everyone's attention from their hands so you don't notice what they're doing with sleight of hand. That's how he snuck the pendant in your bag. Don't stay there if people are cold to you.

Love, Cindy

She and Janet had dinner at the huge wooden table, all fresh vegetables and huge steaks. Jacky couldn't eat the huge meal. She was used to salads and takeout food now. A meal was left near a microwave for Lachlan when he returned. She and Janet talked for a few hours, filling in all the time after when she and her mother had left. Memories came back, such as the teacher who had put nasty comments on her assignment in red ink, saying she was obviously bright in spite of her obvious determination to be different and not fit in. Her mother had been angry about it when Jacky showed her the comment. That teacher, Mr Jones, was a burly man with an angry red face. Jacky had pleaded with her mother not to go into the school to talk to him about the inappropriate comments, which he often made on her work.

'There's nothing wrong with you!' her mother had declared. 'That teacher doesn't have enough to occupy himself in a small town. He's acting like a schoolboy. You are English, like me, with an English soul. There's none of your father in you.'

Jacky had been terrified her mother would go to school and mention things like souls when many of the teachers were harsh atheists who would regard her with contempt. Her mother had long steeled herself against contempt and stoically resigned herself to her fate. However, she had contacted her family in England. Plane tickets were sent to them and they had left for England. Jacky hadn't returned until now. It all seemed so much wilder and remote than she had remembered, while no one had previously told her any of the family history even though it was her history too through her father. That is, until Janet bought out boxes of faded photos that went back to the very beginning of photography. There were old sepia photos of sturdy, spirited Highlander ancestors and distant relations from Scotland. She could see their indomitable spirits and their hope for this new land beaming out of the faded photos. The very first ancestors had lived in rough wooden shacks by campsites near the coast. Maoris had helped them. Later, ancestors were prosperous farmers when the homestead was a fine mansion.

At about ten p.m., Jacky went to bed. In a way, she had found her roots somewhat but it was not the same as really belonging here. If anything, her spirit belonged to the mesmerising lake.

An old uncle living here had told her once, tapping his forehead, 'If you think you belong, you belong.'

She agreed with him but it made no difference in the end if others didn't want you to belong.

The next day, she went exploring. There was an old Art Deco house down a lane surrounded by trees like a witch's cottage in the woods. Ernest, an Englishman. had lived there for a long time now. People said he had worked for the secret service in England and had made enemies who were after him and so he had taken refuge in an out of the way town. If you knew no better, you would not ever guess there was a house hidden in the trees.

Ernest opened the door and invited her in. Jacky was astounded at how old and frail he looked now, with longish silvery grey hair around his neck. The house was still impeccably neat in the English way, so that you might assume he still had a wife. Ernest made a pot of tea in an English china teapot and poured the tea into matching teacups while he spoke about his belief that modern people were at a loose end with no values or goals other than survival and money just for the sake of it while they turned on each other as a substitute for sport or war. They abused work privileges which were slowly being taken away from them because they had no sense of the past in which all their rights had been won at a great cost.

Jacky didn't really like tea but she understood its importance to English people. Ernest took out some very bland biscuits from a biscuit caddy. Jacky left after drinking her tea.

Back in town, she recognised an old schoolfriend, Janelle.

'How are you, Janelle?' Jacky asked.

She hoped Janelle would invite her in to talk about old times but Janelle said, 'Oh, hi,' in a rather forced way and tried to open her gate, which had a stiff latch. Jacky opened it for her.

'I'm escaping from all the tourists,' Janelle explained, implying that Jacky was one of those tourists.

Jacky reminded herself she would be going soon and so it was best to not be friendly with any unwelcoming locals. She made excuses to save face and walked away. She felt she would never have coped with being a pioneer leaving Scotland for the promised land of New Zealand. She would've died, penniless, alone and hungry, on a Scottish shore.

When she walked in, Lachlan was watching TV as usual with empty beer cans on a coffee table.

For once, he spoke to her as if he was used to her around by now. 'What did you do?' he asked.

'I wandered around town,' Jacky replied, without elaborating.

'The local yokels,' he replied laconically, looking a bit like a local yokel himself. However, he had lived and worked in cities for years and so he had more of an urban, casual look and he spoke to her as an urbanised man might do if in the mood.

Janet came out from the kitchen. 'Come into the kitchen,' she said. 'This room is Lachlan's den now. I tell him to clean it up but he doesn't and so it's best to just avoid it.'

The kitchen was large and bright with a scrubbed wooden floor, and light streamed through the windows. There were small armchair-like chairs that were a bit threadbare but clean. Jacky sat down on one and Janet on the other.

Janet began reminiscing about the past to Jacky. She described a town Jacky never knew. Exotic people who weren't just tourists filling in time seemed to pour into the town from everywhere once to settle there. Many people on the run had settled there, like Ernest. The townspeople used to gossip about what the other runaways might have done.

There was a sailor with a Polynesian girlfriend who they guessed probably had a wife back in England. They guessed a few runaways had been in jail and had to move away from everyone they knew upon being released. Small town folk gossiped but no one knew the facts. There was the strange dark couple, Mick and Alanna, whose origins no one knew; maybe they were gypsies or Spanish. Mick was a drunkard and a womaniser. Alanna wrote poetry. The most they revealed was that they had last lived in Australia. They had left as suddenly and mysteriously as they had arrived with a brood of children ranging from very fair to very dark, which stunned everyone even more so than the Maori woman, Rangi. Rangi had married an Irishman, Paddy, and they had boys with Maori features but red hair, green eyes and freckles. The boys worked for their builder father.

'The town must have been interesting then,' Jacky said.

Jacky only remembered school uniforms and the smell of wet wool emanating from them in winter and sarcastic schoolteachers and her mother's mantra about one day they would leave, year after year, until one day they had actually left for good.

'People in the town gave a damn about things then,' Janet declared. 'The townsfolk back then weren't all just chasing after tourist dollars. People came and stayed rather than flitting about here and there around the world.'

'Maybe my mother had a story as to why she came and buried herself here,' Jacky remarked. 'Do you know?'

Janet said, 'I always thought her story was that she fell head over heels in love with my drunken relation, your father. Refined, educated women often fall hard for men like your drunkard father.'

'I suppose they don't know beforehand what potential partners might become when they're no longer courting and romantic,' Jacky said defensively.

'Maybe,' Janet conceded. There had been a time when Janet conceded to no one.

'What happened to all those interesting people?' Jacky asked.
'A lot of them died and many, like a lot of relations you might remember, eventually moved on,' Janet replied. 'Most of our family and cousins all got good jobs in the city. The farmland got sold. Only this house is left like a leftover from the past. The gypsy fortune teller, Tatania, is still alive in town somewhere. She keeps very much to herself. She was a beauty once with long dark hair like a horse's tail. She wasn't a blonde Russian. She's very old now and looks like an Indian with a dark, lined face and pure white hair.'

'I'd be interested to talk with her,' Jacky said wistfully.

'She only occasionally sees anything accurately for people,' Janet said. 'I think she mostly guesses, in a cunning and insightful way, and very rarely she gets amazing flashes out of the blu,e but you may just be wasting your money on her so she can buy alcohol and cigarettes.'

Jacky was intrigued nevertheless and drove off to meet the Russian so-called psychic. She arrived at the cottage, which was a typical old house with gables and a veranda. A large orange cat was sleeping in the veranda. The cat opened one sleepy green eye and carried on sleeping. Jacky was startled when an old woman opened the door before she even knocked. She looked like a charismatic old Indian, just as Janet had said, with a lined, tanned face and glowing white hair.

'Hello. You've arrived,' Tatiana said as if she had expected her. 'Don't give me money. All I can tell you is that you don't belong in this town, even if you were born here. You belong to other lands.' She then firmly shut the door.

'Another cold small town local,' Jacky thought.

She returned to her car. She drove around the town hoping to see some of the interesting kinds of people Janet had told her about but saw only tourists, cafés, a few tour buses and various local people who she didn't recognise. The locals looked as if they belonged, while the tourists did not.

She saw that mysterious boy, Asher, at a bus stop. Some youths appeared to be harassing him, a boy pulling roughly at his jacket. Asher stared straight ahead as if oblivious and shutting them out. Jacky felt indignant. She drove over and told him to jump in.

'Back off, you kids,' she said angrily to the youths as Asher climbed in and buckled the seat belt.

'Is she your girlfriend?' one youth said cheekily.

She realised they weren't really cheeky but more just young and ignorant.

'When he's much older,' she said haughtily to them.

They jeered.

'Really?' asked Asher, sounding a bit pathetic.

Jacky didn't want to hurt his feelings. 'I'm too old for you. Look at all the pretty girls around,' she said firmly.

People always thought she was much younger because she was so short and thin with long, casual hair.

Jacky said no more, driving along the road back to the homestead and stopping when Asher told her where his home was. He got out and walked up a path and indoors.

When she arrived home, Janet came out to give her a message. Jenny had invited her to dinner and said that she was very grateful she had come to Asher's aid. He must have told Jenny to invite her for dinner.

'You may as well go there,' Janet said. 'I haven't cooked anything yet.' She was sitting at the table. 'I meant to warn you,' she said, 'that Jenny belongs to any silly underground group going, Buddhism, meditation, UFOs. She's given Asher silly ideas that he's part alien.'

'That's all right,' Jacky said. 'She's a good person. At least she's friendly. This town needs more friendly people.'

'Her mind is way too blown open,' Janet said. 'That can only happen in the country.'

'In the city, many people's minds are blown permanently shut so no one could ever prise them open,' Jacky said, 'so that they're self-obsessed know-it-alls who actually know nothing.' She told Janet she would be leaving town soon.

'Well, there's nothing much here,' was all that Janet said. 'It's good Lillian took you back to England with her.'

Jacky was silent, thinking even going to England to live had not been smooth sailing. She had been uprooted from all she knew even if she and her mother didn't really belong in the town, both tarred with the same brush as being outsiders, even though she had been born there and had a local father until he died. However, England, her mother's homeland, was just a strange new land.

Jacky went back to her room and changed. She went outside, got into her car and drove back to Jenny's long, low house. She knocked on the door.

Jenny answered. Her blonde hair was shining, newly washed. 'Thank you so much for helping Asher,' she said.

'It's nothing,' Jacky said. 'I was driving home your way. It's all I could do.'

'It's a lot when most people look the other way and do nothing,' Jenny said. 'You learn about these things when you've raised a child like Asher.'

'I was a bit like that once,' Jacky said. 'I know how others just look away.'

They sat around a table laden with bowls of vegetables and salads and a bowl of boiled, new potatoes.

'This is not a dull country town as city folk think,' Jenny said. 'You'd be astounded at the runaways and criminals that come here. A local lady married a murderer on the run once. Luckily, the police tracked him down.'

'Was that Ryan?' Jacky said cynically.

Jenny laughed. 'I really want to tell you an amazing story about Asher,' she said. 'Make of it what you like.'

One night, not long after Ryan and Jenny had become a couple, Jenny woke at night to a light shining in her bedroom. Ryan wasn't at home. He often stayed until late in the city or wherever he went. Jenny had gone to the window to see lights on the other bank of the river. She had crossed the rickety bridge to investigate, although later she felt she had been as if irresistibly drawn to the site. Later, she had confided in friends who thought she must have stumbled into a backpacker's camp and been given a drugged drink. Her pregnancy could have been the result of this strange experience she only partially remembered.

'Why do you think Asher might not be Ryan's child?' Jacky asked.

Jenny explained that Asher had been unusually advanced in reading and in maths and science and just about everything. She realised he also had paranormal skills.

'It all sounds baffling,' Jacky murmured, 'but some children are very gifted. Ryan is super-intelligent and seems as if he has weird powers at times. It is human and not alien even if extra-gifted people can seem weird and off the planet to people not as gifted as they are. It's all just very human.'

Jenny conceded what Jacky was saying made sense and fell silent but Jacky felt she didn't fully agree. Some trauma must have blown her mind wide open to strange ideas.

'I don't trust those counselling, assessor types of people either who have a creepy interest in him either,' Jenny declared. 'I think they could recruit Asher for espionage. I know it sounds weird but security agents used to scout for people like Asher.'

'Maybe they did many decades ago,' Jacky said. 'Surely that doesn't happen nowadays.'

'I think a great many things are just better concealed nowadays,' Jenny declared.

'Maybe,' Jacky remarked diplomatically.

'Asher is drawn to you because you know what it is like to be alienated,' Jenny replied.

'I'm short and thin,' Jacky said, 'and so I look much younger to him and to a lot of people. Asher and I have both lived in other countries. It's not so odd for older people to have lived in other lands but it stands out like a sore toe to certain teachers and fellow pupils when you're at school.'

Asher came back in, fully aware they had been discussing him.

'I'm leaving tomorrow,' Jacky told them. 'Sorry to be so blunt but that's the way it is.'

She just felt once again she didn't belong and never would. That must have been how her mother had felt. Asher looked sad but she hardened her heart. She didn't need a teenager with a crush on her. She said goodbye to them both and returned to the homestead.

The following morning, she drove the little dark blue car down the winding road. The silver lake shimmered on one side like a magic mirror. She could easily imagine a spirit lady of the lake holding up a magic sword like in the legends about King Arthur but there were no gallant knights of the round table here. No lakes in any other land ever seemed as magical as this lake in its shimmering intensity.

After what seemed a long time, she had eventually passed the alluring lake, which finally released its power over her. She wondered if it were this ethereal lake which had blown Jenny's mind so open. She had to return the rental car, board a train and then board a flight back to brash, prosaic Sydney. The interlude with the magic spell of the lake was over.

The Spanish Wedding

Jacky walked through the airport into a hot Spanish summer. She got into a taxi. On arriving, she was hugged excitedly by Cindy the minute she stepped out of the taxi. The sun touched her face and ran down her limbs from an azure sky that was so clear and bright it looked as if it had been polished by diamonds. The street looked dusty and the houses were simple.

She was in Spain for Cindy's wedding to a Spaniard, Josef. Jacky was happy to be there on the Costa del Sol but felt a strong sense of not really belonging. For one thing, she couldn't speak Spanish. She had come from England, where she had been working for a few months, with its soft grey skies and pastel greens everywhere and dark grey streets. She wished she could be like Cindy, who seemed to fit into this hot, vibrant land so easily, but Cindy was a lovable, brash Australian with fluent Spanish and had been living in Spain for years doing an assortment of interesting jobs.

'You must meet Josef,' Cindy excitedly declared. She took Jacky by the arm and shepherded her down the street,

Cindy almost looked Spanish, except her eyes were green and her skin was fair with tiny gold freckles on her upturned nose. She was wiry, agile and short, with dark brown hair that bounced around her face. Jacky was even fairer and shorter with long brown hair, with a red tinge, and blue eyes. She was quiet as if she thought a lot about everything rather than darting everywhere hugging people, laughing, talking and doing things like Cindy.

Over a car with the bonnet up, a dark man with sharp features was talking excitedly in Spanish to another man. Jacky couldn't believe this was Josef. Cindy was always excitedly talking about him on Facebook or over the phone. In photos, he hadn't looked so short, sharp-faced and sly. Jacky supposed she just didn't understand Spanish people and that was why. She had been all ready to utter prepared statements of how lucky Cindy was to marry a tall, dark, handsome Spaniard but the words died in her throat. Men who weren't even Spanish looked more like handsome Spaniards, including her ex-husband. Miami, in Florida, where she had spent some sun-soaked time once, seemed more like Spain with many tall, dark Hispanics. Spain was the recreation country for millions of British who had probably made the locals more reserved and cold like themselves from focusing on British tourists for their livelihood.

She greeted Josef and he nodded and spoke to her rather coldly. They stopped and chatted for a while before Cindy pulled her into a small café. There was the usual European charm of white walls and minimal decorations, unlike the clutter of English décor, and the café exuded a bright, warm atmosphere even though only she and Cindy were sitting at one of the small tables. Through the window, Cindy suddenly noticed a slim, elegant older woman, with jet-black hair coiled into a sleek knot, stop and speak to Josef. They seemed close to each other.

Jacky felt suspicious. 'Who is that woman speaking to Josef?' she asked.

'That's Carla,' Cindy airily said. 'Josef has known her all his life. That's why they're so close and familiar with each other.'

Josef and Carla seemed to be mentally touching but without actually physically touching, in the most sensuous way, but Cindy was oblivious to this covert intimacy. Like many Australians, Cindy did not understand anything that wasn't open and out there, with a lot of noise and talking. She did not understand that men and much older women could be very close indeed.

'Carla looks a bit wild,' Cindy said, 'but she grew up in a cave. Her family were poor.'

Jacky thought Carla seemed mature and elegant rather than wild.

A middle-aged Spanish woman was wiping down tables. In heavily accented English, she declared, 'Carla's family lived in caves during the civil war and after when people were very poor. Carla grew up in a house like you and me. She has an apartment in town. She's a flamenco dancer.'

'Is she a good dancer?' Jacky asked.

The woman, Maria, laughed. 'It is second nature to her now,' she replied.

Jacky could easily imagine Carla totting up in a little book all the tips she received for flamenco performances and storing the money in a strongbox. She had that calculating sort of look in her eyes and would have done well, in a suit, in the corporate world.

Maria bought them strong coffee. Josef, his man friend and Carla disappeared somewhere and Jacky followed Cindy to her tiny flat.

Later, they walked along the public beach. The big resorts that accommodated mostly British tourists owned much of the beaches. The resort buildings towered dazzling white, or pink or a golden hue. Behind them was a lot of tall, yellowish grass growing on a rise where some children played.

'Cindy!' a little boy called out and he and other children, boys and girls, ran to greet Cindy, chattering excitedly to her in Spanish. They ignored Jacky, apart from darting shy glances at her.

Later that evening, they went back to the same café to have dinner with Josef. Cindy explained Josef worked there, among other places, as a chef but he wasn't working tonight. Once they were married, Cindy and Josef would return to Australia, where Josef planned to open a Spanish restaurant. Jacky wondered how much of it would be financed by Cindy but didn't like to ask. Josef and Cindy conversed in Spanish and Jacky felt so jet-lagged she felt as if she was forcing her eyes to stay open and she kept drinking more and more of the sangria, which was sparkling ruby red with sharp hints of a fruit orchard. Suddenly she dreaded this wedding and wished she could stop it but it would be too much like telling a child Santa Claus didn't exist. Cindy, like some Australian women, was touchingly childlike in ways.

Jacky managed to walk back to Cindy's place and sprawl onto the sofa which was to be her bed. Cindy had gone to Josef's mother's place to get ready for her wedding. Jacky had cut it fine, as the wedding was to be tomorrow.

Jacky rose feeling very hung over. The little whitewashed chapel where the wedding was to take place was down the street. Cindy had pointed it out to her. Jacky pulled a sky-blue dress out of her bag. She had a smart white jacket to complement it but it was crumpled from travel and it was too hot to wear a jacket. The blue dress had got crushed but the creases slipped out when she shook the dress, which rustled in her hands. Her white hat was a sun hat which had stripes of transparent material and stripes like white ribbon.

She walked down the road and entered the church. She knew she looked like a demure boarding schoolgirl, being so short and with hair flowing way down her back, especially in Spain.

To her surprise, Carla came over smiling and holding red roses.

'You need more colour!' Carla exclaimed. She pinned red roses onto Jacky's hat and pinned a red rose on her dress.

The music started up from a trio of musicians. Cindy walked in looking very radiant. She wore a ballerina-length white dress with de-mure lace over the sleeves and bosom and had a little white lace hat. The white contrasted with her brilliant red lipstick. Josef's sisters were bridesmaids in brilliant, shiny turquoise dresses that puffed out around them. Jacky wondered why so many bridesmaids wore huge, puffy dresses in bright turquoise or other brilliant colours like hot pink and electrified lemon.

Before long, Josef arrived in a dark suit and his friend from the street the other day was his groomsman.

Jacky's mind wandered off as everything, the service, the wedding vows and the music were in Spanish. She decided she mustn't share her suspicions with Cindy, who would think she was crazy or jealous.

At the wedding feast, everybody, Cindy included, chattered excit-edly in Spanish. Jacky drank a lot more sangria, which was unwise but it helped her cope, at least for a while, with the brilliant sun, the heat and bright colours of Spain that were like a shock to her senses after cool, pastel England.

Cindy changed into a pink suit and she and Josef set off on their honeymoon, which was at another beach area. The plan was that Jacky was to stay at Cindy's flat until she and Josef returned in two weeks' time. She walked down the road and entered the flat. She had an uneasy feeling of intruding when she went into the bedroom. Maybe she would get over it. She reflected on how she and Cindy had met in London, Cindy from Australia and herself a kind of Anglo/New Zealander. Cindy had ended up working in Spain while she had floated between New Zealand, Australia and England and didn't know quite where she belonged any more or if she belonged anywhere at all. She belonged to herself.

The following day, Jacky returned to the café where they'd had dinner because it was one familiar place and the waitress, Maria, spoke English. Maria smiled at her when she entered. Maria was in her forties with a plump build and her hair was styled and curled.

She fussed around giving Jacky advice. 'You should do what Cindy did. She approached one of the resorts and got a very well paying job. She basically helped out where needed as a hostess, on the front desk, doing all the phone and paperwork, and helping as a waitress in the café when needed or working as an interpreter.'

'I'm not Cindy. It sounds too much for me,' Jacky replied.

'It will do you good. You should stay in Spain for a while and you'll lose that English pallor and learn to relax and enjoy life more.'

'What do you know about Josef and Carla?' Jacky asked, to change the subject more than anything.

'What should I know?' laughed Maria.

'They just seem extra close,' Jacky replied. 'Don't tell anyone I said so. I feel terrible asking.'

'You're not terrible,' Maria said, shrugging. 'Everyone noticed that but so long ago no one really sees it any more. It's best to say nothing.'

Jacky ate a buttered roll and drank black coffee.

On an impulse, she walked over to the resort and walked into the foyer of one. They all seemed very alike.

She approached a woman who looked like a manager at the desk. 'Do you need any English-speaking staff?' she asked. 'I'm Cindy's friend. She married Josef.'

The woman, Marta, looked her up and down, assessing her.

Jacky ended up on an afternoon shift. She worked there for a few shifts before returning to England. She would've stayed the full two weeks as planned but just couldn't face Cindy and Josef with all her suspicions screaming at her as if they had a voice of their own.

Two years later, Jacky travelled back to Australia and visited Cindy in Western Australia. Cindy and Josef proudly showed her around their Spanish restaurant in Perth. To Jacky, it didn't look very Spanish. It was very modern for a start, in a new building like a rectangular box with a flat roof and big windows. It was decorated with framed travel posters of Spain. The leading attraction was the flamenco dancer, Carla, promoted as being a kind of gypsy who had grown up in a cave in Spain. Josef had sponsored Carla to immigrate to Australia. Jacky knew it had actually been Carla's grandparents who had lived in a cave, not Carla. The restaurant was on the itinerary of many of the tour coaches and Cindy boasted they made a fortune from the tour coachloads. Jacky imagined most of the tourists would know nothing about Spain and would think the café authentically Spanish.

Cindy and Josef now had twins, a boy and a girl, Joel and Juanita. Cindy was the same bubbly person but Jacky could see she worked very hard; she had turned into a workaholic. Jacky had learned to avoid working for organisations in Australia managed by a certain type of sturdy, athletic blonde woman as they were very exacting of themselves and others. Often, relaxation for them was heavy drinking. Cindy just didn't seem the workaholic type, as she was too charming. However, Jacky suspected Cindy now relaxed by heavy drinking, although it was impossible to know who had drained all the empty bottles. She noticed Cindy putting in long hours, doing all the books, waitressing, handling complaints, taking bookings and generally making sure everything was extra all right. She was worn down very thin. Carla, on the other hand, looked voluptuous; her shiny black hair coiled back, her lips full and sensuous but her eyes wary and a bit shifty. She looked rather self-satisfied. She must have been at least forty but she was one of those ageless people and no doubt dancing kept her figure flawless, and she was very fit. Jacky departed after a week as she had a job in Melbourne to start and Cindy was too busy with the restaurant and her twins.

On an impulse, many years later, Jacky went to Western Australia for a holiday and dropped in on Cindy unannounced. She was horrified at the change in Cindy, who was very thin which huge sad eyes. She had taken up chain-smoking and there were many ashtrays overflowing with butts.

'Cindy? Whatever has happened? You look dreadful!' Jacky exclaimed.

Cindy dragged on a cigarette, thinking before she spoke. She had never thought before she spoke.

Eventually, she slowly said, 'Josef was carrying on with Carla all along. They planned it. Josef got residency in Australia as he was married to me. He organised for Carla to come out on the grounds that her flamenco act was essential to the authenticity of his Spanish café.'

'How did you find out?' asked Jacky, horrified.

'I told him I was going into town for a beauty treatment. I'd got the day wrong and so I came home as I'd nothing else to do. I walked in on them in our bedroom. The most awful thing about it was that they were so passionate and in a world of their own. I realised in an instant that we had never been that close or passionate. It felt like my life was flashing before my eyes while I was drowning.'

'That is so appalling,' Jacky declared. 'They used you in the most cold, calculated way.'

'I'm just staying in our house for now but it has to be sold. Josef is buying out my share of the restaurant,' Cindy said, dragging on her cigarette.

Jacky looked uneasily around. 'Where are the twins?' she asked anxiously.

'It's my fault,' Cindy replied flatly. 'I was always working so hard doing two people's work. That's how we made so much money. Of course, Josef worked very hard too. However, the children wanted to stay with Carla and Josef. She used to babysit them a lot while I was slaving away like Cinderella. I get them on visits. I realised how I had become distant from them as I was always too busy.'

Jacky could see Cindy had finally grown up. It was good to see she had matured from being a trusting, generous, Australian with a touching childlike quality but this tough rite of passage, from her Spanish wedding, had been brutal and it was as if the old Cindy had gone; it was like losing a child.

'I've learned a lot,' Cindy declared. 'There's a new me now. I'm never going to work that hard again or give myself to people. I'm going to enrol in university. It's what I should've done instead of rushing into that Spanish wedding.'

She wouldn't hear of Jacky giving up her job to help her. Cindy said in her new grim voice that it was all her own silly fault.

Jacky hoped Cindy wasn't on the path to becoming one of those harsh Australians women who practised a very extreme form of taking responsibility for their choices in life. They blamed themselves and blamed others for their choices in a very judgemental and joyless way. No man or woman was an island and there was generally much unconscious input from others that shaped choices in life. Many Australians couldn't see they weren't all-seeing, all-knowing gods even if Australian athletes triumphed at the Olympics and on the sports field.

'Don't be hard on yourself,' Jacky said reassuringly.

'Well, I really envied you when you married Ryan,' Cindy said. 'I felt I had to get married too. It's silly when you think about it.'

'Especially silly when we ended up breaking up,' Jacky said wryly. 'I learned from it to really value my freedom from trying to please a man, or please anyone for that matter.'

She was amazed that Cindy had ever envied her. No one envied her.

'Maybe I'm hard now,' Cindy said, 'but you have to stop under-valuing yourself, Jacky. You're a good person and they're few and far between.'

'Thank you, Cindy,' Jacky replied. 'You have always been so kind to me. A lot of people just don't bother.'

Cindy looked a bit like the old Cindy for a moment as she grinned and hugged Jacky. 'Both of us are sadder and wiser,' she declared.

It was some years later and Jacky had returned to live and work in Melbourne, where it wasn't too hot. She was walking in a park one weekend and a busker called out her name. She was baffled as to how he knew her. However, he was playing acoustic flamenco guitar extraordinarily well. Curious, she walked back towards him. Suddenly, she recognised him. It was Asher. She had visited New Zealand in a last-ditch stand to connect with her Scottish pioneering ancestry but it was as if cold English blood, from her English outsider mother, ran in her veins. Asher had been a troubled teenager then and had formed an instant crush on her seeing she looked years younger like a teenager and probably always would look like that, being short.

She sat down on the grass beside him. He offered her his seat.

Jacky told him, 'You play guitar very well.'

'Remember when you said you would be my girlfriend when I was older? Does the offer still stand?' he asked her, grinning. 'You must come back to my place,' he entreated.

He had a small flat off an alley.

'Why aren't you in some high-powered systems engineer job or similar or a CEO?' Jacky demanded. 'You're so brilliant.'

'Brilliance as you call it has brought me no friends and only curiosity and envy,' Asher replied. 'The corporate world and working in a building like a mausoleum are not for me. When an old gypsy taught me flamenco guitar, it was as if I discovered my own soul.'

'I understand,' Jacky replied.

She and Asher had both been born in the same small town in New Zealand and had both lived through the small town hostility towards those who were different. It was extraordinary that they should meet again like this.

'I'd gone back home to Mum in New Zealand when you first met me,' Asher said, 'after Dad went weird again. I'd been living with him in Germany.' He launched into what had happened.

Ryan had taken him to Germany with his new wife, Sophie, and stepson, Damian. One day in Hamburg, Sophie was virtually outside their flat and about to come inside when a thief attacked her, grabbing her bag. Ryan saw but didn't come to help. Luckily, Damian rushed outside to help his mother, dialling the police as he went. The attacker had stopped trying to punch Sophie and take her bag and ran away. The police arrived. A policewoman took a statement and a policeman ran off to try to apprehend the assailant. Meanwhile, Ryan was very indifferent about Sophie's ordeal, which he saw as her problem.

'He goes weird with everyone in the end,' Jacky declared. 'I was with him for a short while. On the one hand, he's super-educated, over-educated some people say. On the other hand, he had picked up bad ways from a party scene in Auckland in old houses where men prayed on young females who were under the influence of drugs and alcohol. There was a lot of violence towards females that was just accepted under a cover of drug-taking, loud music and fun.'

Asher said, 'Sophie left Ryan immediately to stay with an old boyfriend.'

They had told Asher the best thing for him was to return to his mother. Asher had gone back to his mother as soon as he could. Sophie had paid his fare and gave him money.

Asher was taller, as would be expected, and thinner too. After finishing school and dropping out of university, he had left to travel in Europe. He had settled in Spain and learned to play flamenco guitar. He had quickly picked up fluent Spanish. He played in cafés, as well as doing bar and waiter jobs, and busked for tourists, which was very lucrative. He had produced a CD which he sold at busking gigs. He had left Spain and travelled around Australia and had ended up in Melbourne, which had a strong music culture.

Jacky told him about her own occasional travels in Spain. She told him about Cindy's sad, ill-fated Spanish wedding.

'Let's have our own Spanish wedding,' Asher declared. 'We won't be star-crossed lovers.'

She laughed.

'I'm serious,' Asher told her.

Jacky reflected that no men of her own age and generation were interested in her but there would have to be a lot of compromising in a relationship with someone so much younger even if they appeared to be the same age. She suddenly was acutely aware of how lonely she had felt much of her life, with no family except her mother who she rarely saw now. At least Asher and she shared some history of being born in the same home town which no one knew anything about. It was a unique, remote place still, in spite of the tourists, and she remembered that magic lake that seemed like a portal even though common sense told her it was childish to still think of it in that way.

Jacky decided to move into Asher's flat as it had more character, even though he had travelled light and owned very little, mainly just guitars. His flat was closer to everything interesting. She got part-time nursing work. Asher was doing all right from music gigs and busking during the day.

Cindy had moved to Melbourne and was completely immersed in academic studies. Cindy was aiming for attaining a PhD. It was as if she obliterated her memories of Josef and the children they had produced. After all, her children had chosen Josef and Carla over her. The ill-fated Spanish wedding now seemed so long ago like different people in a different world.

Who Wants To Be a Millionaire?

The long, low house was set on the banks of a sparkling, blue canal. Enormous lizards, that Tanya called water dragons, prowled around. The front lawn was a strip of unnaturally green grass and a few shrubs and succulents. The huge boat dominated the canal. It was glittering silver chrome and dazzling white. Tanya hummed and sang to herself as she went about her work. She had dark eyes that were at once shrewd and sparkling. Her curly hair was bleached blonde. She gazed out the window at the boat moored in the canal. She raised her hand over her eyes against the glare.

An old Frank Sinatra song, 'Who wants to be a millionaire?', suddenly surfaced in her mind. She began to jauntily sing the song in a teasing way. Her velvety contralto voice was surprisingly unharmed by her chain-smoking. Her eyes mischievously sparkled and she smiled cheekily.

Her employer, who had told her to call him Todd, liked her to be a bit cheeky now and again as he knew she would quickly become respectful again.

Todd was not the type of millionaire Tanya had seen in glossy magazines, or on TV, with smart cars and young girlfriends. He was old and wheelchair-bound. She did personal care duties and helped him into bed at night. She slept in a small adjoining room off his so he could call her in the night if he needed help. She took him wherever he wanted to go. It was essentially the same as caring for small children and picking them up from school. She had plenty of experience of that and of a gambling, drinking, now ex-husband. It was so much easier to care for Todd.

'Do you fancy my boat?' Todd asked her, smiling in a good-humoured way. 'What say we take her out?'

Tanya excitedly replied, 'We can all handle boats, even Peta my daughter. Her father taught us all, me included. Peta and I don't have boat licences but Michael, my oldest son, does.'

Michael was too much like his father. He already had a record with the children's courts. The job centres got him courses, including getting him into training to get formal boat licences, but he would never hold down a job.

'It's settled then,' Todd declared. 'Your family can come here for a light lunch one day and we'll all go out in her, and Laura too.'

Laura was Tanya's former neighbour from when they were both living in Sydney. Laura had given up a job she hated there and had joined Tanya in Queensland. Todd had allowed her to stay in his home with Tanya.

Laura felt dazed and jet-lagged. Her former home was dust under a wrecking ball, or very soon would be. She had left Sydney in the nick of time. It wasn't long ago but now her former life seemed as if it were a very long time ago as she sat in a huge house waiting to go out on Todd's enormous boat.

Back in Sydney, the demolitions crews started at six a.m. The entire street was being bought, house by house, to make way for developers who were building a long row of McMansions already snaking into the distance. The long road curved up a hill onto a headland from which a panorama of beaches with golden sand stretched on both sides. The vast McMansions were all double-storeyed with huge basements down below stuffed with discarded furniture and other expensive items. It had only been a walk up the road to see a breathtaking view of the sea with a path down to the beach where she loved to walk. The salt air restored her body and mind while soaking into her clothes. She seemed to shed sand from her shoes and hair afterwards.

She was a slim girl with long, light brown hair. She dressed very casually as she had done when she was a student. She sat down on a bench and waited for a bus.

The Blimp, as she privately nicknamed him, had looked expectantly at her when had she walked into the main open plan office on that day she had resigned to go join Tanya in Queensland. She had inwardly groaned when she remembered she was supposed to have a one on one with him this morning. He would berate her for not being bubbly enough even though he and his narcissistic mates were enough to turn milk sour. Her only allies were Jean and Martina but they were women and the Blimp did not respect women. The office consisted of a squabbling, cynical bunch of people on the one hand and very quiet workers on the other hand and neither type were friendly. The extroverts were focused on whatever nasty gossip they could dig up about each other. The introverts just looked knowing and superior. Her life was changed when she read a postcard from Tanya who had moved to Queensland. The postcard had read,

Hi, Laura,

I've been thinking of you a lot. So much has happened. I'm working for a wealthy old man. I stay in his house. He is very kind and says you must come and stay. I told him about your horrible job and he was very concerned. Resign from that horrible place. You can get work here on the Gold Coast. Come up here as soon as you can.

Tanya.

The imminent meeting with the Blimp had decided the matter for her. She would resign on the spot and escape both the wrecking ball and the machinations of the Blimp. Surely she would find work on the Gold Coast in the tourist industry.

The Blimp had smiled his easy, sleazy smile as she had walked in. He had said, 'You don't need to resign. What will you do?'

She felt surprised by his seemingly concerned response for once but realised he was only obeying protocols and was questioning her so he could tick off all the points he had to raise with her on a form. Everything in the office seemed to have a form attached but with an absence of any associated decent human emotions.

She had walked quickly out of his office and sat down at her desk to type a brief resignation letter. The Blimp looked stunned but didn't try to stop her. She realised he had typecast her as someone who would stay on if she were not pushed, being put down every day until she was old like Jean, who he despised, who had only three cats as her back-up.

As she had walked along the beach near her cabin for the last time, the turquoise water frothed with white caps sank and heaved and rolled to the golden shore. It was hard to leave it but soon she would no longer have a home here and would have to move to a unit tower block. Living near the sea had become very expensive in Sydney.

It had all happened so quickly. She had boarded a jet for Brisbane. Michael had met her at the airport. Later, she was introduced to Todd, who was a charming old man in a wheelchair. Now they were all going out on Todd's boat. Her life had changed so quickly.

While she waited in the big open plan lounge of Todd's house, Tanya's family, Michael, Shane and Peta, demurely walked inside. Todd was looking approvingly at the assembled group all ready to board the boat. Tanya was wearing white jeans, a striped blue T-shirt and jaunty cap. Laura was wearing shorts. She seemed a bit overawed but she was a nice girl. Tanya's daughter, Peta, was a very pretty fair-haired girl with curls bouncing around her face and shoulders. Her brothers took seats next to her, They were young, tall and athletic and like night and day, Michael dark and brooding and Shane as easy-going as a summer's day.

Todd was astounded that Tanya should have produced such tall, handsome sons, and such a pretty daughter. He was suddenly at a loss for words, feeling very much on the back foot now, an old man confined to a wheelchair while these tall boys were full of vitality.

'You lot are quiet,' Todd joked. 'Come on. I'm sure you have a lot to chatter about.'

They just smiled, knowing full well older people never approved of their goings-on. Michael only had eyes for the big, beautiful cruiser. He slipped outside to restlessly walk around her. He almost looked happy.

They spent the day on the water, returning sun-drenched, exhausted and blinded by the dazzling sun reflected off the sea. Tanya had invited her older brother, Lenny, to join them on the boat. Laura disliked Lenny on sight. He looked sleazy in a Hawaiian shirt and sunglasses. His hair was thinning. He was paunchy and jowly from too much alcohol. Lenny and Todd were silently summing each other up. Lenny could see Todd was very overawed by the two youths while not being the type to try anything funny such as Lenny did if he could get away with it. Lenny hated Todd for being so good and so rich and Lenny oozed oily charm at everyone.

Todd was too ruled by own inadequacies. He had studied some accounting and law and had gone to work for his father. He had never been handsome and athletic like these two boys. He had inherited the wealth his father had created. He saw Lenny as a petty criminal type who would try bigger crimes if he could. On the other hand, he saw through Michael very clearly, even though Michael was being on his best behaviour. He guessed Michael was the sort of youth with a string of petty offences. He could see he had an ingrained hatred of any authority and he sensed his sullen, angry side. However, Michael's crimes would always be impulsive, on the spur of the moment, and he was not a criminal type, whereas Lenny was. It was as if Lenny's skin oozed sleaziness. On the other hand, Shane and Peta were charming, seemingly quite artless and naïve, or so he thought. He saw that Shane was very bright but would never make anything of his potential, just like Tanya. Later, he told Tanya they could make going out on the boat a regular occurrence but he didn't want Lenny to come with them. Tanya agreed.

Todd had an important meeting one night in his office with his lawyer, Mark, a bright young man. Mark had come out with them on the boat. He was slightly built with longish light brown hair and blue eyes. Laura sat and talked with Tanya in the lounge room with little curiosity over what was being discussed behind closed doors. She knew only a little of Todd's history before an agency sent Tanya to be his personal care person.

Before Todd had ended up wheelchair-bound, a group of youths had got him involved in conversation while walking over a bridge. They had suddenly turned on him, pushing him over the bridge after stealing his wallet. A man walking by had jumped in the canal and saved Todd. He had called an ambulance and Todd was taken to hospital, where he stayed some time being treated for an infection from dirty water in his lungs. He remained frail afterwards. His relations, who he hardly ever saw, seized an opportunity to control his money by having him sent to an old people's home by saying he had got dementia and was too simple and trusting towards riff-raff like those who had turned on him and nearly killed him. There was no telling anybody nowadays that he had grown up a long time ago in a world where it was just normal to greet anyone in a friendly way without fear of being attacked.

Todd appealed to Mark to save him from his relations and from going into a care establishment as if he were a mental defective. Mark had come up with a plan. Todd could marry one of his personal carers. They didn't have secure homes after having divorced abusive husbands. Such women were at risk of joining the multitude of homeless, middle-aged women. Mark's strategy was that he could draw up a contract whereby the nominal wife would inherit the house providing Todd had been cared for in his home until he died. Todd was initially reluctant as he had been married and was faithful to his wife's memory ever since she had died about forty years ago. Mark talked him round.

Mark had met the two personal carers who were rostered on in shifts, Tanya and Jane. Todd had retained Tanya as his live-in main caregiver but Jane was rostered on for Tanya's days off. Mark thought Jane seemed the best candidate for his plan. She was sturdily built and very practical. He knew she had been living in her car for a time before she had settled into personal carer work. Mark ruled out Tanya as he thought she seemed flighty and unreliable.

However, Todd felt as if new vigour had been poured into him during the excursion on his boat with Tanya and her beautiful family. He wished such good times could carry on forever. Todd had asked Tanya to be his wife, who would care for him while he looked after her and her lovely children. His wife had to be Tanya or no one else. Mark wondered if Todd really had lost his senses. He suspected Tanya of being a secret drinker, while her brother, Lenny, had petty criminal as if painted all over him. Shane and Peta seemed pleasant and harmless enough but could they be trusted? Michael seemed like a loose cannon. Mark had a sense of foreboding that Tanya and her brood would easily become too hot for Todd to handle as they all seemed too volatile and ungrounded from a hand-to-mouth existence for too long. But Mark had to give way to Todd.

Todd let Tanya have her special wedding day. He had become very indulgent towards them all. Tanya was thrilled. She was not expecting, as a careworn, divorced mother, to ever dress up again as a bride, in an elegant fitting, white dress with a little matching hat. Lenny hovered in the background looking like a Russian criminal who had smelt out a lot of money waiting to be tapped like wine from the cask that Tanya secretly indulged in. After the wedding, Laura moved into a share house and got work helping in a resort.

Laura attended the wedding but felt very dubious, as it was not a marriage 'arranged in heaven' as they said. She knew by now, though, that too many marriages were definitely not 'arranged in heaven', with depressed wives and abusive husbands who eventually divorced at great financial loss.

Laura felt uneasy when, after just a few months of marriage, Todd unexpectedly died. Tanya was now a rich, merry widow as if crying crocodile tears to please everyone. Actually, her tears were more over the stress she felt at the burden of wealth she had inherited. She had only ever desired a moderately comfortable life and not this. She invited Laura to stay with her again, eager to impress her with her new-found wealth. Tanya had always felt Laura looked down on her as she had had an office career. Of course Laura had always whined about the Blimp, her boss, but wasn't it a norm for people to hate and fear their boss? Laura had been oblivious to Tanya's envy.

Laura arrived one typically sunny Queensland day. The huge boat was gleaming out in the canal in the usual spot. Laura joined Tanya in the lounge room. She was amazed at the change in Tanya. Tanya seemed to have lost warmth and her manner was rather brittle and forced. She had gone from being thin and overworked to becoming quite plump with a round face. Her hair was cut short, permed and dyed a warm caramel colour that set off her dark eyes. She was elegantly dressed in black pants and a pink, fitted top. She now owned a pink Ferrari, parked in the drive. Tanya wore smart, gold high-heeled sandals while Laura's leather sandals were well worn and comfortable. Laura felt miles apart from her old friend with so much wealth and glamour yawning between them now.

Laura was soon regaled with a litany of woes. Michael and Shane were being targeted by drug dealers and women who were either escorts or exotic dancers. Meanwhile, somebody was helping themselves to large sums from her accounts. Laura noticed both Tanya's sons were wearing Tanya's pin number on their hand and so it seemed obvious who was helping themselves to her money. Tanya was frequently too drunk to go to the ATM herself and would despatch her sons with her card and pin. It would be so easy for their disreputable girlfriends to access both card and pin numbers written on their hands while the boys were distracted. On top of theft from her accounts, Tanya's car had been tampered with by unknown people, either her sons or their predatory girlfriends, who imagined themselves being married to her heirs after her death. Luckily, her mechanic friend, Bill, had called by to check out her car. He adored the car and loved fiddling with it and so he had discovered in time that it had been tampered with.

Laura decided that Isobel, an exotic dancer, was gentle and friendly but probably dishonest if she could get away with it, while the escort woman had a mean, steely look in her eyes. It seemed clear to Laura that if you were wealthy, you couldn't trust anyone however pleasant and polite they seemed, and everyone around Tanya was pleasant and polite except for Michael. Maybe Michael was the only genuine one trying to keep Tanya down to earth.

'You always look so young,' Michael had said approvingly to Laura.

She didn't know if he was just flattering her or not.

Tanya confessed to Laura how she had felt completely lost after Todd had died. She had lavished huge sums on her ungrateful siblings but they always wanted more and they were now bitterly jealous and taunted her and nagged her about her drinking and a host of other issues that they hadn't seemed to notice in the past when she was poor and struggling. Laura realised that Tanya's work as a personal carer had given her a kind of stability but as a rich widow she was at a loose end and surrounded with people she could not trust. No wonder she was stressed. She poured out her troubles to Laura, as in the old days, but now they were like a poor little rich girl's troubles and sodden with alcohol. Tanya had turned into an old soak and Laura felt she should tell her to go into a rehabilitation clinic to dry out but was too afraid to speak up. Laura was sharply aware how she and Tanya now had lives that were poles apart. The money had come between them. Tanya's family had changed too and looked scornfully at her.

Laura suddenly noticed a very petite girl with long fair hair who had quietly come in. Tanya mentioned to Laura that she employed this girl, Tracey, to do some cleaning on and off. Laura got up and followed her into the basement area when Tanya was distracted by Michael.

'You must be Laura. Tanya told me you were coming,' Tracey said in a friendly way.

'How do you find it here?' Laura asked, curious.

'I'm not coming back,' Tracey said. 'Actually, I only came back to get something I left behind.' She opened a cupboard and retrieved a bag of clothes. She declared, 'I've heard a lot of rumours and talk that poor old Todd's death was no accident. The alcohol and drugs make them all paranoid. I was actually Michael's girlfriend to start off with but since we broke up they're really suspicious of me about what they think I might know about them or what Michael may have told me.'

'Why do people suspect Tanya of killing Todd?' Laura asked.

'All I can say for sure is that Tanya is too blotto half the time to do anything at all,' Tracey replied. 'She's too clueless to watch her money,

All the con men and sharks are after her and they'll catch her in their schemes sooner or later, just as she caught poor old Todd. Lenny is a creep. He tried to abduct me once but I got away. He's paranoid and thinks I'll dob them all in over something. I don't know much. I'm not here watching them all the time.'

'What has been going on?' Laura demanded.

'Well, for a start,' Tracey said, 'I suppose you heard that someone had tampered with Tanya's car. The boys and Peta have a motive to kill her as they'll inherit everything. They've all been helping themselves to her bank account. It's like Ali Baba and the forty thieves here.'

'We probably should both keep well away,' Laura said, suddenly feeling alarmed.

Tracey said. 'For a while, I was just hoping Michael would come back to me but I don't want him back now. I'm afraid of them now as they think I know too much about them all.'

'What exactly do you know?' Laura demanded.

Tracey explained how a new nurse had left Todd in the sun outside a café while she did shopping. Tanya had delegated her previous nursing duties once she had become Todd's wife. Michael had pushed Todd, in his wheelchair, into a cold windy spot. He had bought Todd an alcoholic drink. Todd had passed out. Michael had then gone to chat up the nurse, who was rather smitten with him. He had told her Todd was fine and they had gone to a bar. By the time they got back to Todd, the damage was done. He had passed out on strong alcohol and was slumped in his wheelchair. Soon after, he had contracted pneumonia and died.

'How do you know all this?' Laura demanded.

'One of the neighbours saw it all happen,' Tracey replied. 'She told me.'

Laura declared, 'If she was there, why didn't she help Todd?'

'She was busy working inside one of the cafés,' Tracey replied. 'She said she was outside when she saw Michael move Todd into a cold corner and come back with a drink. She didn't go outside again until it was quiet, which was hours later. She then saw that Todd was still there out cold in his wheelchair in a cold, windy spot. There's no proof any of it was deliberate, however, or that he was drugged by Michael.'

'What about an autopsy?' Laura asked.

'Peta told me that Tanya was afraid Michael had drugged him,' Tracey said. 'That's why she requested no autopsy and why she arranged for Todd to be cremated very soon after death to protect Michael. All we'll ever know is that Michael and the nurse left him in the cold after Michael had got him dead-drunk. They were negligent but there's no proof of any crime. Lenny's really rattled.'

Laura suddenly remembered that office which she had hated. It seemed very trivial now compared with this toxic paradise Tanya had inherited.

Michael and Tanya were quarrelling and they didn't notice her and Tracey slip outside. They left in Tracey's car. Laura felt too scared to ever go back. Lenny might try to abduct her as he might think she knew too much after talking with Tracey.

One day, a year later, Laura met up with Tracey at a popular shopping mall. Tracey had left momentarily to look in a boutique, leaving Laura drinking coffee at a table outside a café. Laura was astonished to see Michael striding towards her. His dark hair curled over his forehead and there were almost black circles under his eyes. His face was puffy.

'Still the same old Laura,' he said affectionately.

'Well, yes,' declared Laura, voice cool, thinking Michael looked like a drunk now.

'You've always been a good friend to Mum,' he said. 'Come over and talk to her. Why did you leave so quickly that last time?'

She went with Michael over to where Tanya was sitting. Tanya looked thin and wiry once more. Her cheekbones jutted out sharply. Her hair was pulled into a bleached ponytail, no longer elegantly styled. She was chain-smoking, a pile of cigarette butts in a paper cup. Laura was shocked. It was as if a magic spell had been broken and Tanya had fallen back into the jaws of gritty reality.

'It's gone,' Tanya declared dramatically in her velvety voice. 'All of it, the cars, the boat, the house and all of the hangers-on who were like bloodsuckers. They all dropped off once the money had dried up. They'll all inherit nothing from me. I'm glad it's all gone. Michael is all I have left.'

Laura felt like saying that Michael was the worst bloodsucker of them all. He had never paid his way. She wanted to accuse Tanya of encouraging all the bloodsuckers and Michael's bad ways but it would be too unfair as Tanya had been as if sucked into a maelstrom of wealth she had never dreamed of before. She had been totally unprepared for it. She had unthinkingly lavished money on many but nothing to Laura, who felt she had never really been a close friend or maybe they had just grown apart. It wasn't the money, which she would have refused, but it was as if she had been forgotten about by Tanya who was pandering to her new friends.

Tanya explained she had made some very unsound investments with charming salesmen and she had lost everything while the salesmen had escaped with lucrative commissions. Tanya looked very pathetic when she explained all this as if planning to persuade Laura to help her out. Laura knew any handout would go on booze and cigarettes,

Tanya suddenly spotted Tracey walking over to join Laura. 'That girl, Tracey, is a viper!' hissed Tanya. 'I did so much for that girl.'

Laura was aware that Tanya had manipulated and bullied Tracey while Tracey was infatuated with Michael. She realised she would have been treated the same herself if she and Michael had ever been romantically involved.

Laura inwardly shuddered at a sudden vision of her endlessly helping Tanya and Michael out with loans that would never be paid back while Michael was well able to support his mother. The rose-tinted lenses had fallen from her eyes and now she saw them merely as worn-out cheats, gamblers and drunks.

'What have you to say for yourself, miss,' Tanya hissed at Tracey, 'spreading gossip and running off with Laura, my only friend.'

'Sorry, Tanya, but we have to go now,' Laura said, grabbing Tracey's arm and hurrying her away.

'You didn't have to grab me like that,' Tracey protested.

She was much smaller than Laura and Laura's hand had left a red mark on her arm.

They ended up going to another café elsewhere. They reminisced over coffee about how they had each met Tanya and Michael.

'Todd looked like my former nasty boss, who I called the Blimp. Michael had met him and hated him too. The Blimp had white hair bleached a funny yellow and a belly just like Todd, but he was way younger than Todd. The Blimp had got like Todd decades before his time,' Laura declared.

'Todd was nice. He wouldn't harm anyone. He was always polite,' Tracey said, 'not that I saw much of him as he died rather suddenly and suspiciously, as we both know.'

Laura remembered Michael had hated the Blimp especially when he knew the Blimp was giving her a hard time.

'I don't like him,' Michael had said once when she pointed the Blimp out when Michael had come to see her on some pretext at the office. 'There's something rotten about him. He's probably cooking the books or something,' Michael had said.

'Michael is a law unto himself. If he likes you enough, you're safe with him,' Tracey remarked.

'The Blimp was like that too,' Laura said. 'Michael is no worse than the Blimp in that regard. I wonder if he liked Todd?' she added uneasily. 'I'm worried Michael harmed Todd because he reminded him of the Blimp.'

Her hatred of the Blimp might well have carried over to affect Michael too. She wondered if Todd had suffered and died as a result of a superficial resemblance.

Tracey said, 'We don't really know if Michael or any of them deliberately harmed Todd. It just seems suspicious how he died so suddenly when he had been well enough.'

'You did say he died after being got dead drunk and left in the cold all afternoon by Michael,' Laura replied. 'However, Michael is so ignorant I suppose he could have treated Todd that way without any malicious intent behind it.'

Tracey didn't reply.

Laura felt uneasy.

Tracey protested, 'There was no way of you knowing beforehand that Tanya would marry a millionaire, was there? You can't blame yourself. You don't know if Michael had been inadvertently conditioned by you to hate Todd because he resembled the Blimp. I think the best move is that we just stay well away from Tanya and her entire family. Tanya feels she's to blame for Michael being so crazy and that's why she carries him like she does. Its nothing to do with us.'

Laura declared, 'There's no point in Tanya suddenly being friendly to me again now the money has all gone. She'll want handouts all the time.'

'All we really know now is how not to behave if we were ever millionaires,' Tracey declared, laughing cynically.

'I don't think we will ever be millionaires,' Laura remarked.

'Let's head back home now. I'll drop you off at your place,' Tracey said affectionately. 'Let the past and its dead sleep peacefully.'

They hurried back to Tracey's car. Darkness descends quickly in the tropics.

Goodbye to Doll's Houses

Drizzling rain hissed through the forest of greyish eucalypt trees, forming snake-like patterns against a misty sky. Faded orange-tiled rooves seemed to burrow down under a canopy of slippery leaves. One house stood out. It had been painted purple but the intense colour had now faded. The property looked as if it had been transported from Colombia due to the tall rainforest trees crowding around it. Locals called it the drug house. Everyone, including housing officers and the police, stayed well away.

A thin dark girl, Dara, was waiting in a bus shelter nearby, raindrops glistening on her thin woollen jacket and black, cropped hair. The words of one of the newcomers in the area suddenly ran through her mind. 'It's cheap rent to the Housing Authority. You just have to pray neither a gum tree falls through your roof nor a criminal falls on your head! Hear no evil, see no evil, and speak no evil like the three wise monkeys, and you're safe.'

The trees towered over the purple house like a jungle. At least they gave her privacy. She was a squatter there for now but only until she got word from Finn, her boyfriend.

The bus was late. Dara decided to walk, to clear her head, through delicate gum trees that gently sprinkled raindrops on her as she brushed past. Entering a clearing, she climbed a hill. From this vantage point, she could see traffic snaking along narrow winding roads through the bush, resembling flailing, light-studded tentacles of a giant octopus. A vast influx of population, traffic and commuters had far outstripped the scenic, meandering roads that networked the area. Sydney was relentlessly encroaching on this area, like the slow march of sand dunes taking a brash, dry emotional desert with it. Maybe within a hundred years the meandering pretty roads would be wide, straight roadways and pretty gum trees savagely trimmed back from these barren highways. City values would permeate the area like osmosis, bringing dry materialism and superficiality. The city emotional desert would have taken over.

Later on, cold and wet, she arrived back at the purple house, walking down the narrow path. She walked into her room, crouching on a bare mattress, with a cigarette. She looked critically at her current image in a cracked mirror leaning against the wall. Now a spiky crop replaced her thick mane. She wore a gold stud in her nose, and one on her tongue. Silver earrings lined her earlobes. Her gaunt, fragile beauty was as delicate as her silver jewellery and her fragile well-being. She reflected that if there were rats there, they would have been stoned on the hydroponic marijuana plants. Some biker gang members came regularly to tend to the plants. She was allowed to stay in the house by some former associates. She had nowhere else to go. She had done a cold turkey withdrawal in a Buddhist centre. She had learned how to cook vegetarian food, and do intensive cleaning and to serve in their café. There was such an atmosphere of peace there. She had left to make way for other addicts like she had been. She had metamorphosed into her current state of tense fragility.

Finn was an old friend she had met not long after leaving the Buddhist centre. They had got talking when she had contacted her old friends about somewhere to stay. Finn knew the crowd they had all been associated with, beyond the edges of the law. Soon she and Finn would get away altogether from people they knew so well it was dangerous now. Meanwhile, she justified squatting illegally as vandals would break in and wreck it if it were empty. Her former associates, who still rented this house from a public housing authority, were now living in a city pent house, in Sydney, paid for by drug money. As long as the rent was paid, the Housing Authority didn't check up on them.

Dara's cellphone buzzed. It was a message from Finn to meet him in inner Sydney, at Ruby's Café which they frequented. She hurried to the bus, slamming the door behind her, sound echoing in the cavernous house behind her. After a bus and train trip, she was in inner Sydney.

Finn was standing in the shadows of Ruby's Café. The door and windows of the café poured out warm golden light. People walked in and out jostling him, not noticing him in the shadows. Someone asked him for a light, assuming he was outside to smoke a cigarette. The acrid smell of smoke wafted around him. Suddenly, Dara was smiling impishly at him. With her close-cropped hair, and thin jacket over her skinny body, she could have been mistaken for a boy except for the grace with which she moved even in thick rubber-soled boots.

'I'm so hungry. Let's get something to eat,' she said.

He followed her inside. 'I've booked us both flights to New Zealand,' Finn said. 'My passport's still valid.'

'So is mine,' declared Dara. 'Luckily my passport is something I haven't lost or sold. This jacket has huge internal pockets in the lining where I keep important stuff. It's a useful jacket even though it looks thin. It keeps me warm too and keeps most of the rain out even though it's second-hand. It was a good thrift shop bargain.'

They dunked strips of flatbread in thick, steaming lentil soup that warmed their hands and faces as they ate.

'I have nowhere for us to stay,' remarked Finn. 'I'll come back and stay with you. Tomorrow we're leaving.'

'In my squat?' asked Dara.

'Better than sleeping in a doorway,' remarked Finn.

'I want to stay here as long as I can, drinking coffee, relaxing and soaking up the atmosphere,' said Dara, 'before I go back to that dismal squat. After I've been away, it hits me how bad it is, like a kind of darkness.'

They looked around at groups of students and friends, gay couples, lesbian couples, workmates, chatting and laughing. Some young girls defiantly showed a lot of flesh, even though it was a chilly night. Finn could see how their boyfriends noticed Dara, in stark contrast to them all, in plain, dark clothes, her fine bone structure accentuated by her cropped hair.

'I see them all like one brain,' Dara mused, 'with tenuous links and bonds between them all, positive and negative energies, all spinning while tenuous links divide or join their good side and dark sides.'

'I see a lot of people not connected at all,' Finn said. 'They just think they belong.'

After a train journey, they boarded a bus. The headlights illuminated gum trees, like contorted skeletons, pointing fingers at them in the darkness. Finn followed Dara up a muddy track to the purple house.

'I'll check who's there first,' said Dara. 'Wait here, out of sight, behind those trees.'

Finn watched as Dara unlocked the front door and switched on a light. She disappeared in doors. After what seemed a long time to Finn, feeling chilled in the damp trees, she appeared at the door and beckoned.

Finn walked indoors.

'I'll show you around,' said Dara, ironically.

Finn was appalled at the bare mattresses thrown on floorboards, thick dust in some rooms, a hydroponic laboratory occupying the main living area. 'I feel sorry for the people who live in areas like this,' he remarked. 'I've had enough of this life. When I first met you, I was ignorant of what that crowd we were in with was really up to. I thought it was a proper job. I suppose, because I'm part Maori, they just assumed I didn't care what side of the law I'm on. I'm just their errand boy, chauffeur or cleaner, but some things I've seen make me sick. Can I have a cigarette?'

Dara lit his cigarette.

'There was one place,' said Finn, 'a month ago, where they had an illegal crop. A local teenager walking in the bush stumbled upon it. He ended up drowned in the river. A gut feeling tells me my so-called bosses drowned him even though I saw nothing and have no proof. I always had to drive them to places where I shudder to think what they were doing.'

Dara shuddered. 'Why did they get you to drive them around?' she asked.

'It would have made it harder for anyone to trace their movements,' replied Finn. 'Various people would pick them up and drop them here and there but only they knew the final destination. If anyone stopped to check the car, they would ask for my licence, not theirs. I'm so glad I'm getting out of here.'

'Where will we stay in New Zealand?' asked Dara.

'My Aunt Nyree's place. She looked after me when my mother died. I let her know we're coming.'

'What about your father?' asked Dara.

'All he gave me was his green eyes,' remarked Finn, laughing, but his eyes were bitter. 'He left. He was Irish.'

Dara peeled off her damp T-shirt, revealing an elaborate tattoo on her back. The tattoo featured an ornate casket. Snakes writhed from one side while butterflies flew out the other. 'Pandora's box' was tattooed on the casket in Gothic lettering.

'My full name is Pandora. My mother thought it was a name like her name, Pamela. My stepfather changed it to Dara,' she said. 'It symbolises the good and bad in life that people discover.'

'Not much good in the types we've been involved with!' remarked Finn.

'At least my former friends let me squat here for now,' remarked Dara. 'I had nowhere else to go.'

They curled up together and Finn fell asleep. Dara felt reassured feeling his warm body next to her.

'Wake up!' she suddenly hissed. 'A Housing Authority officer is coming up the path.'

'Well, they don't know we're here.' whispered Finn, still half asleep. 'The door is locked. We'll keep quiet.'

There was loud knocking on the door. They heard a rustling sound, as a letter was pushed under the door. Footsteps tapped and died down along the overgrown front path. A car engine started up.

'It's just another letter about how tenants must have a yearly house inspection,' said Dara.

Finn noticed a pile of curled, yellowing letters scattered in a corner, like dried leaves, near the back door.

'They push a letter under the door and go away for another year, generally,' remarked Dara. 'I've heard sometimes the tenant dies. Meanwhile, social welfare goes on paying the skeleton's rent.'

Finn looked horrified. 'Doesn't the government check up on people?' he asked.

'The short answer is no,' Dara said wryly. 'For instance, the housing officers work alone and not in pairs. They get gut feelings about some places and basically keep away for their own safety. I think it's time to go,' she declared.

They stuffed items in backpacks. Together, they slipped out of the house like two shadows.

At the bus stop, they could see the car driven by the housing officer wending its way around the streets, a bright red flash of colour amidst the gum trees.

'She looks very young,' remarked Finn.

'I heard they like them very young and put older people off. That's how it goes,' Dara said. 'It's the way of the world.'

A bus pulled up and they got onboard. Dara reflected at last that she was leaving. In a few hours, they would be on a flight to New Zealand.

The housing officer, Kristin, saw two dark figures board a bus. She wasn't sure if the smaller figure was male or female. A gut feeling told her they were from the house where she had pushed a letter under the door. She had heard all the gossip from residents about the house but she couldn't enter without permission. Many years ago, a colleague had ignored it when the residents painted the house purple and let them plant trees which in a few years became like a jungle. Many people had also reported the house to police, who had nothing concrete to go on especially when no one was ever home. The house, like a faded, garish doll's house, was very much in everyone's too-hard basket.

Kristin had only worked for the housing authority for six months but felt she had built up about ten years of knowledge about how the other side lived only a block or two away from couples who went to work, had children, maybe a dog or cat too, and had mortgages and all the other respectable things.

Kristin pulled up outside Penny's dwelling. Penny had handed in notice that she was leaving, probably just to go on the run from enemies who knew where she lived. Penny had come into the office one day to tell her, shaking in fear, about a man who called himself 'He Whose Name Must Not Be Spoken.'

Penny had looked taken aback at meeting Kristin, a young blonde girl like herself but even younger, who clearly knew very little about life on the wild side. Penny had burst into tears with no coherent information about the predatory, nameless drug dealer. Kristen's boss had just laughed contemptuously when Kristen told him about the situation. Kristen knew they had to not get emotionally involved but it was impossible to not feel concerned about Penny even though it was up to Penny to go to the police to report on the predators. Meanwhile, the police wanted the housing officers to evict criminals. They couldn't without a police report on the criminal activity. It was an unwinnable situation.

A kind policewoman had come to the office one day to explain to the housing officers that the police had to go on hard facts, names and verifiable information, and incoherent babbling about someone whose name could not be spoken was not a hard fact. Victims were too afraid to dob criminals in to the police as they might be harmed by the criminals. They often knew very little to tell anyway. Even if they had a name, it would most likely be false. Kristin was stunned when, a few weeks later, Melissa, a petite, demure blonde, asked to see her, babbling incoherently to her also about the same person. He probably had a kind of harem of women who he controlleder with illegal drugs. Many attractively presented women who were tenants of the properties had drug habits, although you would never guess it just to look at them. It probably took years for them to end up like emaciated skid row addicts.

Kristin pulled up once more outside the property Penny rented to do a pre-vacancy inspection. She was amazed by a group of women, with ugly expressions, hanging around outside the property. They were thin with sunken faces and lank hair.

As Kristin approached, they suddenly stepped aside and smiled politely saying, 'Hello, miss. How are you?'

In the city, no one had called Kristin 'miss'.

The group of women who had first had ugly expressions reminded her of school bullies who suddenly assumed fake smiles over ugly expressions if a teacher approached, politely saying, 'Hello, miss' or 'sir,' and leaving their victim be until the teachers had gone.

Kristen knocked on Penny's door.

Penny answered, looking like a frightened deer, with huge terrified eyes. 'It's you, honey,' Penny declared in relief, hugging Kristin, who wondered who on earth Penny had been expecting with such dread.

Kristin commenced the house inspection but it was impeccable with a wonderful, retrospective atmosphere of clean, faded print curtains and old-style wooden furniture painted cream.

'The house is perfect,' Kristin declared, filling in the standard form that was completed prior to the tenant vacating.

Penny was poised smiling but then nervously rushing to windows.

'Who are those ghastly women outside?' Kristin asked. 'They look like hyenas.'

'They are hyenas,' declared Penny. 'When I've gone, they'll come in and take everything and wreck the house to give the impression it was me who wrecked it.' There were tears in her eyes. She was pathetically eager to please Kristin.

'That is terrible,' Kristin said, 'especially when you've made it such a lovely home.'

'He whose name I dare not speak thought it was too,' Penny declared, 'until he got carried away with little Miss Squeaky Clean Muffet, Melissa. I heard he got tired of her too and rearranged her face. She has to have reconstructive surgery now. The ambulance took her to hospital just last night.'

Kristin felt horrified. She could do nothing about the situation, which was a police criminal matter. She had checked all the boxes on the form, as was her duty, and had to leave. Only Penny herself could appeal to the police for help but, like all the victims, she was too afraid of repercussions.

Outside, Kristin walked down the path and the group of women once more moved away to let her through, but once she had got into her car, they all moved together as if circling and lying in wait again, like hyenas.

Back at the office, she related what had happened with little interest from battle-hardened colleagues.

'Her boyfriend would've got all those women addicted and near destitute paying for drugs while she was his pet,' a workmate, Alan, explained. 'He probably gave a lot of their stuff to her and they'll be going in to get it back plus interest. It's just another day on the job for us at Housing,' Alan added.

Meanwhile, Dara and Finn were already in New Zealand.

Melissa came into the office one day with a reconstructed, sharp little face, like a mouse, with dark eyes and her hair now a natural light brown and straight. Kristin hadn't recognised her at first.

'I know you were really worried,' Melissa said, 'so I've come in to show you my face is all right now. The doctors fixed it.'

'You look very pretty,' Kristin said awkwardly.

Melissa had then dashed outside like a nervous cat before Kristin could think of any wise advice.

Penny's older sister, Lorraine, had come in to the front desk to tell her Penny was in jail.

'I think she's safer in jail,' Lorraine had remarked wryly. 'I know you worry about them all, darling, but we all know you can only do your job. You should go to technical college and do a course and get out of this dump. It'll only get you down.'

Kristen smiled wanly. She had been studying part-time. She was close to graduation now and close to getting a job in information technology.

Eventually, the police arrested He Whose Name Must Not be Spoken. They followed a trail of information to the purple house and raided it, smashing down doors to discover a hydroponic marijuana crop. The purple house was auctioned off as it was beyond 'economical repair' to clear the jungle around it and to fix the modifications done to turn it into a marijuana factory.

Soon, Kristen would resign and get a proper job away from the doll's houses of disadvantaged young women, who would become just a memory to her.

The Immigrants

Roseen and Donald had immigrated to New Zealand from England. They had met and married in London. Originally, Roseen was from a village in Ireland, while Donald was from Glasgow. Donald was fair-haired and ruggedly built. Roseen was petite with wavy, blonde hair. They had rented a small flat up a hill in Wellington with glimpses of the sea. It seemed to them everywhere in Wellington was up a hill and the strong winds were as keen as a knife.

They soon hit troubles. Donald was going out every night and drinking to drown his homesickness. Roseen packed a bag and left him. She had got work as a kitchen hand in a hostel for hospital workers and trainee nurses. Roseen felt almost as if she were at home in Ireland when she dished out enormous meals, as there was such a variety of fresh, top-quality vegetables and big juicy cuts of meat with lashings of gravy. She was aware of strange looks and funny vibes but assumed she must expect that as an immigrant in a strange country. She tried her Irish charm on everyone but it was not safe out of Ireland. Many people were suspicious and envious.

One day, a laundry worker, Christine, had collapsed, slumped over a trolley in the corridor. Roseen noticed her face was ashen pale and her legs seemed weak as if she couldn't walk. There were student nurses bustling everywhere but oblivious to this woman who washed and starched their uniforms. Roseen wondered if Christine had deliberately positioned herself where there was the most traffic of trainee nurses coming off shifts, who might notice her and help. She might as well not have bothered as it was as if she were invisible to the chattering trainee nurses.

Roseen asked Christine what was wrong and Christine weakly replied it was nothing.

'I'll get some help for you,' Roseen said brightly. 'Don't worry, dear.'
She lightly touched Christine's shoulder and Christine flinched.

She went to Hilda, the woman in charge of all the hospital workers, and persuaded her to come and look at Christine. Hilda summoned hospital staff, who arrived and took Christine away on a trolley. Later, they heard Christine had emergency surgery that night but had pulled through fine. Roseen had saved her life.

Later, a pretty Maori girl, Moana, had quietly come up to Roseen and informed her there was a plot led by a rough-looking girl named Queenie, who was going to attack her that night. Moana explained the other girls had dropped out of the planned attack after Roseen had helped save Christine's life but Queenie was mad and was still going ahead with the attack on Roseen.

'Why ever would they do that now?' Roseen had asked, shocked. She wondered if Moana were a bit crazy.

'Queenie is very jealous,' Moana replied. 'All her friends really like you now because you smile and speak to everyone, even if your accent is funny, and you saved Christine's life and Queenie is jealous over that. She thinks you think you're too good.'

'But that's what we Irish are like,' exclaimed Roseen. 'Christine was obviously very ill. Anyone could see that. I helped her as any decent person would.'

Moana said, 'Those trainee nurses are stuck-up and in a world of their own. They should've noticed Christine had taken very ill but they didn't. We laundry workers are invisible to them like the dirt under their feet. You noticed Christine, though, and helped her. You must leave immediately. The attack is planned for tonight.'

Moana hurried off to start her shift, leaving Roseen wondering what kind of land she and Donald had immigrated too, where a kind act was so out of the ordinary and had provoked a planned attack. She finished her shift, as that was the right thing to do, but her heart began to pound in spite of herself. She went back to her room to collect her bag and a few things.

As she walked down the corridor, she looked back to see Queenie charging at her down the corridor with a mad look in her eyes. Luckily, the elevator doors opened and closed in the nick of time, a chink allowing Queenie's maddened eyes to appear momentarily to Roseen before the doors closed and the elevator descended.

Queenie raced down the stairs to resume the chase in another corridor. Roseen began to run. She noticed an enormous frozen fish defrosting on a trolley. She picked it up and hurled it at Queenie. It struck her and seemed to bounce off, momentarily stopping her headlong charge. A pool of water from the defrosting fish splashed at Queenie's feet and she slipped, sliding along the floor before keeling over in a fat, blubbery heap.

Roseen kept running. She got to a bus stop but the bus wasn't due for ten minutes yet. There was a red telephone box there. Roseen suddenly crazily wished she were like Dr Who and that the box was a Tardis that would whisk her away back to London. The only number she knew was Donald's. She rang him desperately.

'Hello, darling,' declared Donald. 'I've missed you so much. Are you coming home now?' he hopefully added.

'Donald, I'm in trouble. A crazy woman is after me. She tripped over but she'll be back. I'm in the bus shelter outside the hospital but the bus isn't due for ten minutes.' Roseen broke into tears.

'Do you have anything to thump her with if she comes near you?' Donald asked.

'I threw a frozen fish at her,' sobbed Roseen.

'You need a shark, love,' declared Donald, 'not a ruddy frozen fish. Don't worry. I'll be there!'

Donald raced outside and hailed a taxi and told the driver, a Polynesian man, the situation and told him to put his foot down hard and he'd pay him double. The taxi driver willingly obliged. They were near the bus shelter in no time at all. He gave the driver a handful of notes.

'No need for that,' the driver, Sam, said kindly. He gave a lot of the notes back. 'Take her out tonight with this,' he said. He drove over to the taxi rank and watched to see what happened.

Queenie had spotted Roseen at the bus stop and knew the bus wasn't due just yet. She stopped her headlong charge. She was a bit winded by now and sauntered, limping a little as she had banged her knee when she tripped over the fish.

'That's her! She's limping now,' Roseen declared frantically to Donald.

'Don't worry, my love,' Donald declared. He seized a sharpened stake, which had been supporting a rose bush, out of the gardens bordering the hospital building. He charged at Queenie with the stake like a Celtic warrior.

Queenie stopped in her tracks and ran back the other way. She managed to break into a run with Donald on her tail. Donald chased her around the front of the building.

A visiting party of dignitaries, men and women, were coming down the front steps after a tour of the hospital. They all stopped and stared at first Queenie running by and then at Donald following behind, holding a sharpened stake. Donald met their startled eyes. He thought quickly and walked over to a garden, where he thrust the stake in the ground and made out he was tying a shrub to it.

'He's a very enthusiastic gardener,' the hospital official adlibbed to the visiting party, wondering what on earth was going on.

'He must be. He's running to do his work,' a bemused male dignitary murmured, his eyes on the garden where Donald was bent weeding. 'It's a very fine garden,' he remarked for something to say.

'Well, yes,' the hospital official replied, 'because of such dedicated gardeners.' He racked his brains wondering who that gardener was.

The dignitary's eyes followed Queenie, who had not stopped running.

'She's taking exercise,' the hospital official adlibbed. 'This jogging craze has affected everyone.'

'Well, she needs to lose weight,' the dignitary remarked.

Donald thought Queenie might be on her way around the corner to head back to attack Roseen. He brushed dirt of his hands and hurried back to Roseen.

Roseen was in tears. 'You haven't killed her, have you?' she moaned. 'You'll go to jail and then what will become of us?'

'I threw my spear at her,' Donald declared, 'and it ran her through like a pig.'

Roseen almost fainted, her worst fears realised.

Donald laughed. 'I'm just joking,' he said, hugging Roseen. 'Heaven knows, though, what I would have done if I had caught up with her. I'm just amazed at how fast a fat woman like that can run.'

'Fat means nothing,' Roseen said shakily. 'Our convent school top athlete was a huge, fat girl like that. Anyway, she had you behind her and not a lot of nuns.'

The Polynesian man was peering at them from his taxi.

'Come on, lass. We're going home,' Donald said. He took her by the hand and led her to that same taxi.

The Polynesian man, Sam, grinned broadly at them. 'You take her out tonight,' he said. 'You were like a warrior with that stake. You're like my warrior brother.'

He dropped them off at the flat. Donald gave some of the notes back but Sam wouldn't take them. He kept telling Donald he was like his warrior brother.

They went upstairs to their tiny flat.

'Wellington is worse than Glasgow,' Donald declared. 'Anyway, I've got news for you, my darling. I've been offered a job in a country town but I was waiting for you to come back before I said yes.'

'How did you know I was coming back?' Roseen asked.

'I knew,' Donald replied, pulling her into his arms.

Donald rang his employer to accept the job.

They went by train to a little country town of quaint art deco build-ings and houses set in a valley surrounded by blue coloured mountains. Silver rivers ran down from the mountains and snaked across the val-ley,

'Saints alive but it's like the village where I was born,' declared Roseen.

Donald told her he had put a down payment on one of the art deco cottages. It was surrounded by flower gardens and fruit trees. There was an adjoining field.

'We can keep a cow and hens, like in Ireland,' Roseen declared.

Deep down, she felt she would never leave this house and village, just like the Irish village where she was born, even though she knew Donald would always be a bit crazy and into too much drink. At least he had defended her and would stick by her. He had saved her and that was good enough.

Donald had a job in a big warehouse in a neighbouring, bigger town. In the village, they soon met an assortment of immigrants from Scotland and England and even a Russian woman who claimed she had the second sight. If they were in England and met these people, they would probably never have become friends but they were all strangers in a strange country and this drew them closely together. Roseen would never have thought her best woman friend would be a Russian, Tatania, who was not a typical fair Russian. She had long coarse black hair like a horse's tail on the Russian steppes.

Their neighbour was Harry, a blond, handsome English man who had jumped ship and left his wife in England. Harry lived with a Polynesian woman, Melly. He was always in fights at the pub over drunken men calling him a pommy poofter or a whingeing pom. If Donald was drinking with him, they all left him alone. Roseen knew little about Scotland but her two Scottish women friends, Fiona and Kirsty, were very kind and caring people a bit older than her. They all helped her if Donald was crazier than usual.

Roseen gave birth to a baby girl with a mop of copper hair who she named Ashleen. It was a difficult birth and she could have no more children after that. She had only wanted two children anyway. She didn't want to be a brood mare, pregnant every year, like her mother and aunts.

Her Russian friend, who she called Tatie for short, always made dramatic predictions. 'That one will be a runaway,' she predicted about Ashleen.

'Well, she won't be running for a good while yet,' Roseen had laughed.

It made sense that two immigrants running from unsympathetic family and all kinds of things would produce a runaway not confined by borders.

'Enjoy your time with her,' the psychic had said forebodingly.

But no troubles dawned yet on the two immigrants' horizon. Any troubles were many years away in the future, where they belonged, and they lived for each other and for each day.

Meeting the Relations

Roseen was half awake. She was lying in the bedroom in the Irish village where she had lived in her youth until going to London to study office skills and then had gone to New Zealand with Donald, a very handsome but rather crazy Scottish man she had met in London. It had been a whirlwind and crazy romance leading to a crazy marriage and a crazy young daughter, Ashleen. After a long drawn-out compensation case, during which he had become like a mad bear, Donald had been paid a handsome lump sum. His health, spirits and capacity to buy spirits had remarkably recovered and he had paid for her and Ashleen to visit her family in Ireland. A friend had eked out the money in online transactions to make it a mercifully short visit to family followed by travel on to London to meet friends there.

It had been a rather gruelling day with her devout mother and aunts probing into why Roseen had only had one child. If that wasn't bad enough, it had got worse with one aunt saying Ashleen was only a scrawny runt with red hair like a bonfire. She had noticed Ashleen silently seething, which was a foreboding sign in her father. Roseen suddenly woke up worried as she could hear dragging sounds in the adjoining bedroom, where Ashleen was supposedly sleeping. Roseen threw back the covers and rushed to open the door. Ashleen was packing.

'Where are you off to?' Roseen demanded.

'To London,' Ashleen replied. 'I'm not spending another day with these awful relations.'

'I'm coming with you then,' Roseen declared.

Ashleen knew nothing about London.

'When daughters run away, their mothers don't come too,' Ashleen declared.

'I've noticed that,' Roseen said wryly, 'but this time I'm coming too. I don't want to miss the fun, if you could call it that. I don't want to be left here on my own.' She dabbed her eyes.

This rattled Ashleen, as Roseen knew it would, as Ashleen thought her mother weak, clueless and needing protection.

'Oh well, you better come too,' Ashleen conceded.

'But how are we going to get to the station?' Roseen asked.

'Michael will drive us,' Ashleen replied. 'We've worked it out.'

'He's only fourteen,' Roseen declared.

'But he can drive. He drives his father's car regularly,' Ashleen replied.

'I bet his parents don't know,' Roseen remarked.

Ashleen didn't reply.

The first few days had just been too much for Ashleen. Her mother had always told her to be proud of her red hair as it came from her Irish ancestors. Her parents were both blond and so her hair hadn't come from them and chances were even her father probably didn't have red-haired relations too. Red hair just lurked in the Celtic gene pool popping up suddenly on a baby's head to astound their parents and relations. She had entered this big, grey stone farmhouse expecting to discover a clan of redheads only to be faced by what seemed to be an enormous brood of her kin, of all shapes, sizes and ages but mostly very overweight with that nondescript dark hair that isn't really black, pasty skin and blue eyes that seemed to roll back in their heads in disapproval of her. They had the look of schoolchildren who were bottling up all their rude, rowdy behaviour and tricks they pulled on others once the grown-ups had gone, only most of these were the grown-ups. One of the clones, as she saw them, had told her she had a bonfire on her head. She felt like asking them had they stuffed cushions in their clothes to make their backsides so fat or had they eaten the cushions but had outgrown stooping so low. She just wasn't interested in them and their petty remarks and then they turned nasty, accusing her of being a snob.

Roseen left a note on the dressing table telling them all they had received an urgent message from London and had to leave immediately. They crept out of the house to where Michael was waiting in the car. They were all silent as he drove past fields bathed in moonlight, the sky a deep indigo blue. He carried their bags onto the platform. Roseen slipped him some money. They had a group hug and then he left them. He melted back into the darkness and drove home.

Once they arrived in London, they went to the house of Roseen's last employer, Doctor Fitz, where she had been a receptionist. Dr Fitz was a short, slight man with fine fair hair now thinning on top. He wore glasses with metal rims and they magnified his blue eyes so that they looked like goldfish in a bowl. The practice was downstairs in the big, Victorian house he lived in. He had welcomed them both with open arms, telling Roseen she was as pretty as ever and her daughter was beautiful too.

Roseen joked that he must be part-Irish, not Jewish, to be so full of blarney. They all laughed. He was a widower now and he begged them to stay. The receptionist had not come that morning and so Roseen instantly offered to fill in for what had been her old job a long time ago by now. All the old patients were overjoyed to see her.

After a few days, she had offered do her old job for a while to help out before returning to Donald. Dr Fitz declared he wanted to make her his new wife. Roseen was astonished at how many of her former beaux were now divorced and now they all came out of the woodwork. Roseen looked much younger than her age, She had a neat figure even if she was not tall and her blonde hair looked as lustrous as ever. She pointed out to Dr Fitz that her husband would object if she married him. All her old beaux remembered the handsome Scottish man, Donald, who Roseen had married before leaving with him for New Zealand. They all knew he had a drunken, crazy streak but had said nothing about it to her at the time. They had not fought very hard for her then and Roseen decided she was not going to bother with them now.

Somehow she and Donald had clung together in a strange country, New Zealand, where only they had some understanding of each other.

By now, there would be like a huge, craggy, uncomfortable rock gone from under her feet if Donald were no longer there, while no one would fill in the huge gap left by the rock. Whatever his faults, Donald had always supported her and Ashleen. He actually agreed when she blithely told him over the phone she was going to help out good old Dr Fitz for a while. He had trusted Dr Fitz. Little did Donald know that Dr Fitz had proposed to her once, a few decades ago by now. However, his family had pressured him to marry a nice Jewish girl who had since died.

Ashleen felt bored and at a loose end. She decided to go to Glasgow to meet her father's relations. Aunt Joyce was first on her list and the last. She had found herself on a grey-flagged path outside Aunt Joyce's terrace house while Aunt Joyce had stuck a crazy face with mad blue eyes between the lace curtains while accusing Ashleen of being an imposter who had come to rob her.

Suddenly. a girl with coal-black hair and mascara, wearing tartan tights, appeared and spoke to her. 'It's afternoon. Joyce will be really stuck into the drink by now,' the girl said.

She told Ashleen her name was Megan. She was very sympathetic when she heard Ashleen had come from New Zealand to connect with relations from the old country. So far, it seemed like the old and very crazy old country. She was very keen to return to the new world which was her home.

'Ye've come all this way,' Megan said in a lilting accent, 'and the old bat is trying to drive you away and drive you crazy. It's a disgrace.'

Ashleen learned that there had been a feud for as long as Megan could remember between Megan and her six brothers and Joyce and her menfolk. No one knew what had originally caused the feud by now or when it had actually started.

'We'll be your cousins,' Megan declared. 'We'll show you a good time. Come and stay with us.'

Megan told her brothers when they came home about what the old bat Joyce was up to now. Megan had a plan. 'We'll have the biggest party at the pub, with a big notice up, "Welcome Home Ashleen", and Joyce will be jealous for the rest f her life over it. She'll never forgive us for poaching her niece from the Antipodes,' Megan declared.

'I don't want to make things worse for you,' Ashleen said apologetically.

'It'll be worse for her,' Megan declared.

And so a week's carousing began at the old pub with a band and a banner welcoming Ashleen, proclaimed as their cousin. Ashleen felt she had to contribute to the cost. That whole week was like a blur of cigarette smoke, alcohol, smoky rooms and the loud noise you only heard in pubs. Finally, Ashleen was able to slip away and get a train back to London. She texted Megan to tell her she had to see her mother before she got a flight back home.

Megan texted back, 'Take care, cuz. Stay in touch.'

She got back to Dr Fitz's place at four a.m. and flopped into bed. She was sound asleep until what seemed like an earthquake was happening. It was her mother shaking her.

'You smell like a bonfire and reek like a brewery. There are black circles around your eyes and your hair is matted. On top of that, your father rang. His sister, Joyce, found his phone number, after all these years we've been in New Zealand when she never rang him once, and she told him some wild story about you drinking all night and day with hoodlums who gave all her sons black eyes and broken noses over you. You seemed to be under the delusion they were your relations and not his sister. You have a lot of explaining to do.'

'They're my blood brothers and sister,' Ashleen said, her voice still slurred.

Roseen dragged her from bed to the shower and turned the cold water on. It hit Ashleen like shards of ice and she squirmed and protested.

'That's the kind of shenanigans your father would get into,' Roseen declared. 'I always knew you were more like him than me, just to bedevil me I suppose, and add to my troubles.'

Ashleen stood in the shower blue and shivering, water sluicing off her. Roseen enveloped her in a huge white towel, cocooning her like a mummy.

'Go back to bed now and tell me all about it when you're properly awake and sober,' Roseen conceded, her voice a lot kinder. 'That Joyce was always crazy. I told your father that.'

Ashleen fell back into bed. She gradually stopped shivering and fell back asleep.

Everything was quiet when she finally dressed and went downstairs. Ashleen got to talk to her mother over lunch and explained what had happened as best she could about how Joyce thought she was a fraud and had come to rob her. Megan had felt sorry for her and had taken her in and offered herself and her brothers as relations in spirit.

'In alcoholic spirits,' sniffed Roseen, 'by the smell of you. I understand. They were good-hearted and helped you. They could have robbed you, a young girl thousands of miles from home with no family.'

'You're beginning to sound like Joyce,' Ashleen remarked.

'I know she's a crazy old thing,' Roseen said.

'Anyway, I'm sick of the old crazy world,' Ashleen declared. 'I'm a New World person. I was born in New Zealand. I'm going home as soon as I can. I'll go back to Australia again – there's more work there and better paid too.'

'You've seen nothing of the culture and history here,' Roseen protested.

'I don't want to know more,' Ashleen declared. 'The Highlanders were forced off farms and driven to the New World. The Irish were allowed to starve during the potato famines and driven to New York. That's all I need to know about the Old World. My Old World relations treat me as if I'm a New World barbarian. That's all I need to know.'

She was able to get on a flight to Australia within a week.

A few weeks later, Roseen received a letter from Ashleen. She momentarily was too afraid to open it, wondering what trouble Ashleen had got herself into now.

Hi, Mumsy,

I'm just letting you know that Dad has got into a right old funk about you staying on to help Dr Fitz. I think you have stayed on there a bit too long and Dad is totally aggro and wasted over it. Remember when you used to send me to that nice old Catholic woman down the road to stay for a few days? Her hair was grey and she had umpteen kids and grand kids. This was because Dad had got so crazy you thought I'd be safer staying there for a few days. Well, that's how bad Dad is now. I think you ought to stay with Dr Fitz for ever. I'll come and visit you as long as I don't have to meet with our ghastly relations.

You don't know this but I and Dr Fitz had a long talk and he asked me about what Dad was like and if he was good to you. I pretty much filled him in on that. I think that's why Dr Fitz asked you to stay on and help him for a while. Dr Fitz told me his parents had broken you and him up. He married a Jewish girl but she died soon after you had gone to New Zealand with Dad. I think Dr Fitz still loves you. I think you should stay on with him as his partner, if you know what I'm getting at.

Let me know,

Love from Ashleen,

Your wild colonial daughter.

Ashleen deliberately omitted from her letter that she had told her father that Dr Fitz had asked Roseen to marry him once and that he had always loved her. She had also informed him that Dr Fitz's wife had died long ago.

Roseen, when she read this letter, was torn by many emotions and memories that welled up and she began to cry. First of all, she had been stunned at how easily she just slipped back into her former life of being on the front desk for Dr Fitz. It was almost as if she had never left, had never married Donald and never given birth to Ashleen. She had done office refresher courses in New Zealand, courtesy of a job centre, to re-train so she could support Donald and Ashleen while Donald was out of work. However, she was unsuccessful in getting work afterwards. She could work with computerised systems now and Ashleen had sat by to help her initially. Many of the older patients recognised her, which was very touching. They brought in their family photos of their grandchildren to show her. They brought in cakes they had cooked for her.

She loved the little village in New Zealand where she and Donald had settled. In her memory, she smelt the green grass and saw the blue hills rippling on the horizon. Some hills had glistening snowy caps in winter. The rivers were so pretty how they rippled along, bright blue in summer but mostly grey, as New Zealand is a wet place with a lot of grey skies. However, it had suddenly dawned on her that New Zealand had never really felt like home, especially as Donald was so unpredictable. To most people, she remained known as 'that Irish woman'. It was a jigsaw and she was the jigsaw piece that didn't fit in anywhere.

Dr Fitz noticed her tears. 'What is wrong, Roseen dear?' he asked, alarmed. 'Is it bad news from home? Is Ashleen all right?' He had heard of Ashleen's ill-fated attempts to connect with relations from Ashleen herself as Roseen was tight-lipped about any trouble.

The tear-stained letter had fallen on the floor and he quietly picked it up without Roseen noticing. 'Roseen, I should have married you years ago,' he said. 'My wife Sarah died, as Ashleen says in her letter. She was very depressive and overdosed one day. It was too late by the time I'd finished seeing patients.'

'I'm so sorry to hear that,' Roseen said between sobs.

'I think Ashleen is right,' Dr Fitz said, touching her arm. 'We should be partners just like Ashleen says. We don't have to worry about a proper wedding and all that, do we?'

'Oh, Fitz,' Roseen said, too overwhelmed to speak. She always called him Fitz or Dr Fitz. 'You aren't just joking, are you?' she asked.

'No. I'm not,' he replied.

'Well, we can't just pick up where we left off,' Roseen said shakily.

'Well, we didn't ever really start,' Dr Fitz said.

'I think you used to hold my hand,' Roseen said, laughing a little.

'You are funny, Roseen,' Dr Fitz said. 'You always cheer me up.'

Roseen shakily laughed.

'I'll give you time to think about it,' Dr Fitz said.

And so Roseen stayed and Dr Fitz became just Fitz and they were like two lovebirds.

He wasn't exciting like Donald but Donald was too exciting, and she felt she was growing too old for excitement now. Furthermore, she felt she had really come home at last.

The Predator

The cavernous interior of the old brick church seemed warm and mellow, and light streamed in shafts through pointed Gothic windows. There was a stained-glass window at the back, with jewel colours which were dazzling in the sunlight. The old church was in the heart of a busy shopping district and had been taken over by the council and converted into a market with stalls people could rent at a low rate.

Many passers-by dropped in. There were many stalls set up, including grandmothers selling jars of home-made jams and pickles, cakes and biscuits, while young women sold soy candles and incense. There were stalls selling arts and craft, run by both sexes. The stalls looked pretty and colourful, younger women stallholders wearing colourful, flowing clothing and jewellery, which added splashes of vibrant colour. There were stalls for all kinds of pre-used goods. Tarot readers had little stalls, at opposite ends of the hall, and there was a busker outside, guitar case open in front of him.

One stallholder, Patricia, stood out, as much in appearance as by her intense, malevolent glare in Gail's direction. Patricia was wearing khaki cargo pants and a plain yellow T-shirt with a collar. She had long blonde hair flowing down her back and a fringe, a little girl type of hairstyle that made some men feel protective. Patricia's stall was up and running and stocked with glossy brochures and leaflets to promote the cause of endangered animals, dolphins and other creatures. Like the buskers, she had a container for donations.

Patricia had been very demure when Gail processed and granted her application but once her stall had been approved, Patricia seemed to view Gail as an obstacle rather than the person who had pushed her application through. Most customers were polite when handing in applications but some would quickly become abusive once their application had been granted. From time to time, Gail would catch Patricia glaring scornfully at her, like an enraged creature in a lagoon. Patricia's gaze was lingering and vindictive.

Later on, Gail mentioned it to James and that she felt a bit frightened of Patricia.

'Anyway, nothing can be done about a menacing glance. Just watch her,' James had cautioned her.

Gail replied, 'I can't help but wonder what she's really up to.'

As if on cue, Patricia turned and smiled bewitchingly at James.

'She seems fine to me. What a lovely smile,' remarked James.

'She's just putting on innocent airs because you're here. She probably realises I've mentioned how she glares ferociously at me,' protested Gail.

'I think you're imagining it,' declared James, gazing towards Patricia and rewarded by another bewitching smile.

'That's the story of my life with female enemies,' sighed Gail. 'If ever a man is by my side, who might at least give me some emotional support, my female enemies smile at him and the man just thinks I'm crazy.'

James said. 'Maybe she just needs you to smile at her and take an interest.' He walked away.

Gail felt he just preferred to avoid awkward feminine emotions in both herself and Patricia but she accepted his advice. Maybe she had looked too serious and Patricia had misinterpreted it. Gail smiled sweetly at Patricia and was almost mentally almost knocked off her feet by a ferocious glare now that James was only a small figure in the distance. Deciding not to give up, she walked purposefully towards Patricia, who suddenly looked nervous, to ask her in a friendly way about her stall.

'I'm taking it to markets up and down the coast,' Patricia said defensively. 'There are too many good animals being put down while worthless humans live and breathe.'

'What are you going to do about it?' Gail replied in what she hoped was a reasonably helpful way.

Patricia was silent and still as if considering it. 'People will see what I do about it,' she muttered vehemently.

Her mood seemed steely and vindictive in contrast with the other woman stallholders, who were a flowing mix of emotions, gloomy, aggressive or light and happy. There were few complaints and accusations.

Gail picked up a newspaper. She noticed an article about a series of random murders up and down the coast. The person who committed the murders must have had access to vet supplies as a lethal drug was injected into victims such as was used to euthanise animals.

She showed the article to James. 'It's Patricia who's doing these killings,' she declared firmly. 'She's a vet nurse and has access to lethal medications and I know she's psychotic. I can see it in her eyes.'

'She's a psychotic blonde – just my type,' James laughed cynically. 'You're being melodramatic, Gail.'

'I'm reporting my suspicions to the police,' Gail declared.

'They won't take you seriously,' remonstrated James.

'See you later,' declared Gail, hurrying out the door.

She parked near the main police station and walked in. A middle-aged police officer, with a surprisingly fresh face, came to serve her. She got the impression he was shrewder and saw more than it would appear from his open face. She showed him the newspaper story and declared that she had a suspect. He grudgingly gave her a form to fill in.

'Thank you for coming in,' he remarked kindly when she handed the form back but she got the impression he did not take her seriously.

She did not go straight out but hovered just outside the door, out of sight.

She heard him remark to a colleague, 'It's the same with every crime reported in the paper. People read about it and come in reporting their neighbours, or people they've fallen out with, or strangers in the area and people they don't get on with. I'll file it away.'

She walked back inside. He was startled.

'It's not like that,' she declared. 'I have a strong hunch. Will you investigate it?'

'We have hunches too,' the police officer remarked. 'They often prove to be wrong. We need hard evidence. Don't put yourself at risk investigating this matter,' he added, as an afterthought, as if he at least half believed her hunch. He told her his name was Barry and gave her a card with a number for a direct connection to him but she walked away feeling they would not take her seriously.

A week later, she was sitting in her favourite spot on the back veranda. Flowering shrubs and bushes grew thick on the lawn behind the veranda. James had said he would join her later.

She heard someone lift the latch on the gate and tread on the gravel but did not pay much attention. She suddenly looked around in horror to see Patricia behind her, arm raised and holding a syringe. Gail dropped her coffee cup in shock. She was even more astounded to see James suddenly leap forward and grab Patricia's arm in a vice-like grip. Patricia moaned in pain. He dragged Patricia's arms behind her back and wrestled her to the ground.

Luckily, Gail had the presence of mind to shoot a video clip of Gail holding the syringe in her raised arm as James had tackled her. Gail fumbled for the card Barry had given her and rang the number, heart pounding.

Finally, Barry answered.

'Come as quickly as you can!' she declared. 'My boyfriend is restraining Patricia and trying to prevent her sticking a syringe into us!' She explained where she was and how to get there.

It seemed an age but suddenly two police appeared and she had to go through the whole story again.

At the sight of the police, Patricia seemed to go limp and smiled bewitchingly at them, laughing, the syringe falling limply from her hand into the grass. Gail was half expecting the police to get it all wrong and think they had to rescue Patricia from James's grip on her.

Luckily Barry, whom she had spoken to originally, arrived. Maybe it only seemed that way but he seemed to walk slowly and react as if in slow motion.

'The syringe is in the grass now!' Gail declared to him. 'But look at the video on my tablet. It shows she was trying to attack me with the syringe!'

She hadn't even time to look at the video clip herself. Chances were it only showed their shoes and a broken coffee cup.

'Get cuffs on her,' Barry ordered as if in a slow, disjointed, old movie. He gingerly put the syringe in a plastic bag.

'You've touched it!' protested Gail. 'Won't you contaminate the evidence?'

'It'll be fine,' Barry said reassuringly, not looking at her.

The police hesitated, as if not sure. Finally, they put handcuffs on Patricia, who was now smiling demurely, and took her away. Barry stayed to take statements. He seemed to ask the same questions over and over in different ways. She couldn't see exactly what he wrote down but it was very brief, as man notes tended to be, even though he had asked many questions.

Gail felt strangely energised. She wondered if this was abnormal. Her cheeks were flushed with excitement.

James stood there impassively while everything in her world seemed to have slowed down but herself and her beating heart.

Patricia was eventually charged with murdering a number of people by creeping up behind them with her lethal syringe filled with a drug used to euthanise animals. She had been trying to draw attention to how good animals were put down but worthless human beings were allowed to live.

At her trial, the judge made a speech about how many people were activists for animal rights and they were exercising their right to opinions in a democratic society, while Patricia was an extremist, a terrorist, with no respect for the law or for the lives of the innocent people she had killed.

Patricia was diagnosed as a psychopath. She was jailed and taken off the street.

The Jar in the Chimney

Amy entered her mother's bedroom and saw her ashen face on the pillow. Her mother had had died all alone.

At the granite Protestant church, with the grey granite tombstones at the rear, it was a funeral day of sleet and frozen tears on the day her mother was buried.

After the funeral, Amy had stayed home from school to look after her baby sister Helen, and a younger brother, Sonny, as he was called.

One night. she had heard tapping at the window. Two drunken men peered in the window, calling out to entice her to open the door. Amy was only twelve but instinctively she knew that the men, even though their voices were genial with alcohol, intended to harm her. She hid under a table, shivering with fear, hoping they would think no one was home. Her father was at the pub as usual. He had taken to the drink after his wife had died.

Suddenly, Amy heard a loud, drunken singing of the Irish ballad 'Danny Boy' in the darkness.

'It's her daddy,' said one man in alarm.

'You're not worried about him, are ya now?' declared the other man. 'He's always so drunk since his stuck-up Protestant wife died that he'll think we're Father Christmas and invite us in!'

'I'm going, man! Come on!'

Amy heard them running away. She waited until her father was sober before she told him what had happened.

'I'll notify the police,' he declared, grey eyes blazing in his thin face. He had become thin and delicate, his eyes like bright coals in his thin face.

Amy had heard women in the neighbourhood say, 'Her father has got the tuberculosis. He'll be joining his wife soon in the Protestant cemetery.'

Later, the police had come around and asked her questions. Amy heard them, in another room, saying to each other, 'It's against the law for children to be at home without the care of their mother, or some other woman. Their father has hit the bottle now and isn't looking after them.'

Amy wanted to run in and deny it but she knew it was true.

Finally, a welfare worker had taken baby Helen over the channel to relations of her mother in England. The boys were sent to some relations they had hardly ever seen as their mother had disapproved them and thought them rough folk. Many years later, Amy was told the boys had been neglected and made to sleep on hay in a barn. They had to work hard and were dressed in dirty, worn-out clothes like rags.

A policeman bought Amy a ticket and put her on the train to go and live with an aunt she had never heard of who owned a tailor's shop in Belfast. Amy's name was pinned on her so her aunt would know who she was. She was told to wait until her aunt arrived. She was overwhelmed by the vast railway station full of strange people who were all rushing along. She hadn't realised people could be so different from each other. It seemed a long, cold, frightening wait before her aunt arrived. She was a tall, middle-aged, stern-faced woman. Her eyes looked hard and mean to Amy, who was grieving for her gentle, pretty mother. She told Amy to follow her. Amy had difficulty keeping up.

The first few hours were like a blur of confusing people and unfamiliar places. Her new home was nothing like the comfortable farmhouse where she had grown up, where there was a big vegetable patch at the back and flower gardens at the front. The small tailor's shop, opened right onto the street, with other shopfronts all down the street, which seemed to have no end. The living quarters were at the back and upstairs. Amy's bedroom was at the top of the stairs. It had bare floorboards with only a threadbare rug. There was a disused fireplace.

Aunt Edna had curtly lectured her, 'You'll have to work here to earn your board and keep and learn how to be a domestic help. Times are hard. When you're older, you'll be able to get work as a domestic with well-off families in Belfast. I had to run this tailoring shop for my father when he became sick. He wanted your good-for-nothing father to come here, train as a tailor and run the business but your father let us down. So I had to learn to be a tailor and do the books. I can put off the woman who comes in and you can do her job. It will save me the money for her wages. You should be grateful I took you in.'

'But I want to go to school,' protested Amy. 'Mum told me I had to go to school.'

'They're a nasty bunch of brats at school. I'll teach you what you need to know and the vicar will help. We'll turn you into a fine domestic. That's all you need to know, as you'll just get married and have children.'

Edna looked quizzically at her as if judging her for the marriage meat market and decided Amy was pretty enough to attract a husband. Amy felt like a failure already, being one of those girls who were denied an education and thought only good for domestic chores and bearing babies.

Amy met the vicar and his wife at church. The church was very like the church she had gone to in the country. It was a grey, Gothic style Episcopalian church that was frightening somehow. The vicar wore grand robes and was serious and pompous but his wife, Rosmary, looked very young and smiled at Amy a lot. Amy saw a lot of them, as she went to church regularly with her aunt.

The vicar preached a sermon on Saint Patrick one Sunday morning. 'The ancient Celtic people enslaved Saint Patrick,' he declared, 'but after many years the good lord allowed him to escape. He was converted to Christianity. The first thing he did after conversion was to go back to his former masters and preach to them. Such was his loving and forgiving heart. He taught the Irish that Christians didn't take slaves.'

Amy was fixated on this part of the sermon about Saint Patrick being a slave once. The rest of the sermon seemed just like a distant murmuring.

After the sermon, Amy found a chance to timidly approach the vicar. 'Please, sir,' she said falteringly.

'How can I help you, little girl?' he asked her rather sternly.

'I'm a slave like Saint Patrick was,' declared Amy. 'I have to work without being paid and my aunt won't let me go to school.'

'Your aunt is a spinster,' replied the vicar, 'and so you must be patient with her. She took you in because she heard you were keeping your father's house spotless and doing your best to care for the baby. You're very lucky she took you in.'

'I'm not allowed to have a fire in my bedroom,' protested Amy, 'and there are only bare floorboards like ice in my room.'

'Well, you'd be in a pickle if your bedroom and the house went up in flames, wouldn't you? Many houses are set alight by children playing with fire,' declared the vicar.

'But I'm like a slave!' protested Amy. 'Like Saint Patrick.'

The vicar chuckled. 'You must work hard and obey your aunt,' he said. 'Orphans go to relations to work for their board and keep. That's just the way it is. You must be grateful to your aunt that she took you in. It could be so much worse for you.' He looked down at her pleading face, his eyes softening a bit, before he went to talk to more important people who made big donations.

Amy had more success with Rosemary, his young wife.

'I'll ask my husband if you can come and help me, dear,' she said. 'I'll tell him the housework is too much for me and I need you. I'll tell him I only want you as I trust you and not anyone else he might think of. I'll pay you what I can out of my allowance.'

'Thank you. I would love to help you. You don't have to pay me,' Amy declared, her face lighting up.

Amy loved the days she spent with Rosemary and wished she could live there all the time, even if she had to do the domestic chores. Rosemary was not much older than her older sister, who had immigrated to Canada.

By now, Amy was virtually running her aunt's house and running errands, taking parcels to people of new suits and jackets. The first time she went out on errands, she got lost. She was very frightened. In the end, a policeman had taken her home. Her aunt was very cross and had scolded her. Her education consisted of sermons in church and copying pages from books from her aunt's schooldays long ago. She learned to read but her aunt couldn't teach handwriting and her writing sprawled every where as if trying to run off the page, reflecting how she longed to run away. Her aunt gave her clothes cut down from her own clothes or made from remnants left over from customer's orders.

The years rolled by, all much the same, until Amy was sixteen, when she and Rosemary noticed men putting up a poster.

'It's a poster about immigrating to New Zealand,' said Rosemary. 'It says COME TO NEW ZEALAND – A LAND OF MILK AND HONEY.'

The poster depicted a pretty, plump young woman, with short wavy hair, holding a snow-white lamb, in a green pastoral scene. The young woman looked uncannily like Amy, with short, waved, brown hair and rosy cheeks. A good-looking young man, in an open-necked shirt, was in the background.

'That's what I want to do,' declared Amy. 'It's my only hope of escaping from Aunt Edna.'

They studied the small print on the poster.

Rosemary declared, 'I'll talk about it to the vicar tonight.'

Amy thought it odd how Rosemary always referred to her husband as the vicar and not by his name. Maybe it was because he was so much older than her.

The vicar and Rosemary found domestic jobs for Amy among various people in the church, so she could save to pay part of her passage, while the British government would sponsor the rest as they wanted to dump the orphans and the needy far away in the colonies as the cheapest solution to the problem of the poor.

'I won't let her go,' Aunt Edna had protested, saying, 'There are cannibals in New Zealand. A young girl can't go to the ends of the Earth by herself.'

'She's a good, sensible young girl,' declared the vicar. 'God will look after her. Immigration to the colonies is the best opportunity for young people like her.'

The money Amy had saved disappeared from a box on top of her chest of drawers. She went in tears to the vicar, telling him her aunt had confiscated her savings. He handed over a few notes from his wallet. Amy did more work for people in the church. She hid the money she was saving in a broken, blackened jar this time and hid the jar high in the disused chimney in her bedroom. Her fate, and the future of any descendants she might have, rested on a broken jar hidden in a chimney.

The vicar took Amy to a justice of the peace who signed the consent forms on her behalf, seeing her aunt had refused to give consent. Her passage was booked and paid for. The day of departure drew nearer and Amy could hardly contain her excitement, which she had to hide from her aunt as best as she could.

After what seemed like eternity, the day of departure arrived. She went to the port with the vicar and Rosemary with her suitcase, which she had left with Rosemary for safe keeping so her aunt would not be suspicious upon seeing her go outside with it. She had packed the few photos she had of her mother and family and all her sister's letters from Canada. She had not told her aunt this was her day of departure as she feared Aunt Edna would lock her up so she would miss the boat.

'My aunt will come later,' she demurely told the vicar and Rosemary.

The big, black ship dominated the dock. Amy felt both excited and afraid to see it. The ship would be her home for weeks.

'I don't think your aunt is coming, Amy,' said the vicar anxiously.

Rosemary and Amy exchanged winks behind the vicar's back, and hugged each other.

'I'll never forget you both,' declared Amy, tears flooding down her cheeks.

The vicar advised her, 'New Zealand is the best chance for a young girl like you, in a brave new world away from the troubles of Ireland. You must go and do your best. Don't give up going to church now, will you.'

Rosemary was grinning from ear to ear. 'Yes, I'm sure we've done the best thing by helping you. We've outsmarted that old fox, your aunt,' Rosemary declared.

For once, the vicar did not reprimand her.

The last boarding call came and visitors had to leave. Suddenly, they were tearful.

'God bless you,' the vicar said.

Rosemary hugged her and then they were gone, disappearing into the crowds.

Before long, the deafening foghorn sounded and the ship headed out into the grey, heaving ocean and into the unknown, destination New Zealand.

Amy soon became friendly with a jolly group of Irish girls on board, all excited about a new life in New Zealand.

'I'm going to marry a farmer!' declared Maureen, a pretty brown-haired girl with short, waved hair.

'I've heard there's no winter there,' declared Brigid. Bridget was freckled and more serious than the others. She had to leave as she had too many brothers and sisters now in the family home.

They all admired Amy's pretty clothes. Amy did not tell them most of her clothes were hand-me-downs from Rosemary. She let them think she came from a proper family like them, with father and mother, brothers and sisters. Most of the young girls were immigrating because they had too many brothers and sisters at home and the older ones had to go somewhere to make room for them. They and their parents had desperately high hopes of a much better future for young people in the far flung, exotic colonies. They would send their parents money to help raise the younger children.

Amy remembered the excitement of the tropics. She and the girls marvelled at white, coral beaches, palm trees, and black people who called them 'missy' and sold them delicious tropical fruit such as they had never dreamed of before. Amy never forgot first biting into a juicy pink and green watermelon.

This was in contrast to the shock of Wellington, which seemed to be all narrow streets darting into forbidding green hills, and icy winds that sucked her breath away. It was nothing like the pretty pastoral scene on the immigration posters. Wellington was eerily like Belfast with grey skies and shrieking seagulls. There were the same sleazy men about in the streets trying to seduce her, attracted to her pretty innocent, open face.

The merry, giggling girls, with their brave hopes, were reduced to tears, as miserable as Wellington's rain, to bitterly discover that New Zealand was in recession too. There was no work for them.

'The poster calling us to immigrate was a wicked lie!' sobbed Maureen. 'There's no work for us here. There's no so-called milk and honey! We were tricked!'

Kindly but firm officials had settled the girls in a stark hostel where they were allocated food rations of cheese and bread until they could find work. Amy had hated cheese ever since. The very smell of cheese brought back memories of their dashed hopes. The other young girls wrote tear-stained letters home. Their folk sent money for their passage home, and one by one they departed back to Ireland, except for Amy. Amy vowed she would never give Aunt Edna the satisfaction of saying 'I told you so!' Furthermore, Aunt Edna might coldly refuse to take her in again seeing she had outsmarted her.

Amy despaired of finding anywhere in Wellington like the pretty pastoral scene on the Emigration posters. However, at last there was a turn in her luck when an immigration official advised her about a nanny job in the country. From the train window, Amy saw for the first time the green fields of New Zealand dotted with plump, woolly white sheep and frisky lambs.

The glowing references from the vicar and Rosemary landed her a nanny cum domestic job with a bank manager and his wife, John and Elizabeth Clark. Amy was very happy with how informal and friendly her employers and New Zealanders were in general. They were as nice as the vicar and Rosemary. Although the vicar had always been a little pompous, he was a kind man at heart. She was treated with respect, while bosses in Ireland would have treated her as one of the lower orders, rubbing in that she was only a servant. Furthermore, New Zealanders were so ignorant back then, on the other side of the world, that they all thought she was English. She had gone to church so much when living with her aunt that she had ended up speaking like the vicar, who had been educated in England.

Elizabeth was sweet and naïve. She was in awe of anyone from the old world. She admired Amy's pretty dresses that Rosemary had handed down to her, in the latest English fashions, and begged Amy to borrow them. In return, she lent Amy her jewellery to wear to church, and on her days off. When she discovered Amy could bake cakes, she minded her baby herself, while Amy baked cakes. Elizabeth licked the bowls and wooden spoon, like a child. The bank manager beamed at big plates of yellow cake and cream that Amy had baked, and devoured everything like a hungry schoolboy.

Amy met Philip on a day off at a church picnic. Amy had found the young men at dance halls drunken and overly passionate. Knowing the so-called facts of life from her childhood in the country, unlike many innocent young girls at that time, she fought off the young men's ardent embraces and decided to avoid dance halls. She went to the church picnic with another young girl, Susan, who was also a nanny. As she sat on the grass, the soft green grass showing off her plump pink knees, while the sunlight bathed her peaches and cream complexion, she drew one dark-eyed young man, Philip, to her like a bee to honey.

Philip was short with the chubbiness of early middle age, which made him look rather cute. He had curly dark brown hair and his face was unlined.

Philip and she chatted, Amy giggling a lot.

Later, Susan advised her, 'You're a young girl, Amy, on your own with no mother and father in a strange land. Your best hope would be to marry Philip, even if he is a lot older. The dashing young men aren't ready to settle down. They'll just string you along and try their luck on you. You're doing all right to go for Philip! I heard his father is wealthy and buys a house for his sons and daughters when they settle down and get married. The young ones are a bit wild here compared with home.'

And so Amy and Phillip had quickly married in a registry office, before they had really got to know each other. Amy wore one of her smart, cut-down suits and a silk blouse. She wore a brooch her mother had given her once. Amy soon learned Philip did not believe in churches, after the horrors of the First World War that he had fought in as a young boy.

He told Amy he supported the left-wing labour movement. 'We need a government to help ordinary working men and women,' he told her.

Amy confided in him how her Aunt Edna had used her as slave labour.

However, he just laughed and Amy realised, in disappointment, that like most people, her new husband had assumed Aunt Edna was merely very strict, and had expected Amy to work in the home like a respectable, dutiful daughter. Rights at work were, in his opinion, the prerogative of men, not daughters and wives.

Philip had been an ace sniper in the war, marking out Germans who had killed his friends and relentlessly hunting them down. Short, wiry and unnoticeable, blending easily into shadows, he had survived the war physically untouched, while the tall, athletic, flamboyant men of the movies and of digger legend had stood out, making easy targets. His wounds from the war were mental.

His grandmother had taken in orphaned grandchildren, his cousins. She had sent for them to come over in a ship from Scotland. They had been a bit of a handful as they had run wild when their parents died. The family obviously had a soft spot for orphans and so Amy fitted in well enough.

Amy was well schooled in domestic chores, and so the house and meals all went smoothly. When Philip was in the throes of his shell shock and depression, he did not seem to notice her and so she just kept quiet, waiting for it to pass. She always comforted herself by thinking that even if she still just did all the chores, as she had done for Aunt

Edna, it was at least in her own home. His father had bought a pretty villa for them with a field next door for a garden. They had given them old furniture they didn't want any more and many household goods. Although they were not rich, Amy was keenly aware of how lucky they were in the hard times of recession that had followed the Great War. She had always been taught nice girls obeyed their husbands and had babies or else how would the world go on if women did not do their duty and have babies.

Amy never forgot how her fate had pivoted on that broken jar in the chimney where she had hidden her savings from her aunt so she could immigrate to freedom in New Zealand. She told the story to her youngest daughter, who she nicknamed Sissy, her oldest sister's pet name, who was the only one who was interested in her stories of Ireland.

Sissy wryly concluded that Amy didn't entirely escape from her aunt. She carried her aunt's family genes in her gene pool. A few of Sissy's siblings were hard-headed and cold, just like Aunt Edna, and as a result they ended up quite prosperous but not as generous or kind as Amy, who was more like her mother. Sissy conceded that at least Aunt Edna had taken Amy in. Amy had been reduced to a Cinderella-type of life but at least she had learned domestic work to earn her living and to succeed as a housewife.

Everything came down to who had the upper hand and that was very fluid in modern times compared with the era Amy was from. However, her mother's story of the jar in the chimney was always an inspiration when her back was against the wall, reminding her that if she thought big and had a plan she could make it all work out in the end.

(Based on my mother's true story of running away from Ireland.)

Micky's Story

Micky had always hated her name. She was dark like her father, who she hadn't ever seen. He had died in a mining accident in Victoria before she was born, before the First World War had started. She was supposed to have been a son named Mick after him and so her ever practical mother had simply added Y to Mick. She vaguely remembered her early years and knew that they had been very poor. They had lived in a roughly constructed cabin that was wallpapered with newspaper for insulation.

All that changed when her mother, Eileen, had married the cook, Ron, who worked for the mining company. She remembered him back then as a huge man with a big belly and red face from the heat of the oven. He had a big nose and a huge bristling moustache. Her mother had been small and pretty with fair hair. Ron had taken her and her mother to live in a neat, pretty house, with a red- tiled roof, in Mosman in Sydney. He earned a lot of money as a cook. She couldn't remember where he had worked in Sydney but presumed it was cooking for some institution such as a hospital or prison.

Before long, she had a brother and sister, Owen and Nancy, who seemed to have always been so much taller and sturdier than she was. It was humiliating to always be regarded as the youngest child because she was short.

Micky had accepted Ron as her father only to get a rude shock one day when Ron came home with a beautiful china doll in a pretty costume which he gave to Nancy. Micky had waited for him to somehow produce a doll for her too or to tell her he would buy one for her later. He made it clear that Nancy was his blood but she had been another man's child and he would buy her no doll. Micky felt full of rage and resentment. She got one of Ron's cooking knives when nobody was around and beheaded Nancy's doll. She was discovered in the act by Nancy, who was very upset. She told her father. Micky was severely reprimanded and sent to bed without tea. She liked to think her mother had told Ron that it was cruel to buy a doll for Nancy but not for Micky but she felt somehow that had not happened. Her mother was a bit scared of him and very eager to please him as she and Micky had a good life now with Ron. Nancy and Owen had always looked up to her, however, as she was the oldest. They were lovely to her.

She was ten when the First World War had erupted. Ron was exempted from the war as he was deemed too old. He was middle-aged by then. He continued working as a cook and the war years were very comfortable for them. There must have been shortages but she hadn't been aware of it. She was bright at school and so was selected for a grammar school for bright girls like herself.

After leaving school at fifteen, she got office work with a shipping company. It was a fun-filled time between the two world wars. Skirts were short and young people wanted fun. The cinema was very popular then and the screens were filled with glamorous actors like Errol Flynn, a swashbuckling Australian, Clark Gable, Charlie Chaplin, Vivien Leigh and Greta Garbo among so many stars. She had been short and plump but still had a lot of boyfriends. They would cuddle in the back seats and she'd go home covered in flea bites as the dusty, musty seats were a breeding ground for fleas even though the cinemas were very elegant art deco establishments. A musician would play the piano before the luxurious red curtains rose before the movie. Her mother used to tell her she was lucky all she got from the movie was fleas, referring to over-amorous young men who got girls pregnant. The movies were called the pictures back then but were nicknamed the flea and itches because of the fleas.

Micky had been happy working for the shipping company and hadn't met a man she wanted to settle down with until she met an Irish sailor, Bernie, at a dance. He had a long, narrow face and red hair. It wasn't his looks that captivated her but rather his gift of the gab, and he was charming and courteous. He told her she reminded him of Irish girls with her long, jet-black hair and blue eyes. By this time, Micky had decided she was too old at thirty to attract a partner. She was a lot more serious by then and wore her long, dark hair up. They had a whirlwind romance and got married in a registry office. Of course Ron had paid for a beautiful wedding for his daughter, Nancy, but not for her as she was only a stepdaughter. They had a honeymoon in a cheap beachside hotel. No children followed. Her doctor told her the grim news that she could not conceive. She had an irrational superstitious fear that it was because she had chopped the head off her sister's doll.

One day, she fell down a flight of stairs while carrying in the washing. After that, she fell pregnant in rapid succession, boy then girl, boy then girl and boy then girl. Her doctor told her the fall downstairs must have shaken something into the right alignment so she could fall pregnant. It was as if she had literally fallen.

World War Two broke out and Bernie was called up by the navy to go to war. He survived the war but never returned home. Later, she found out a lot of men had simply not returned home. They had met other women, in foreign lands, and simply decided not to return to their wife and children. Micky thought he had probably decided to go back to Ireland. She knew nothing about his family in Ireland or what part of Ireland he came from. Micky hated him when every day her children, especially the older boy and girl, who remembered him more clearly, plaintively asked if Daddy was coming home today. They kept going out to the gate to look down the road for him.

Finally, she and the children moved north to rent a house on a lake. The rent was much lower out of Sydney. There was an abandoned boat on the shore and the sea was in the children's blood. They stopped asking about their father and went out on the boat every day, coming home late every night. She could hear their laughter before she saw them.

One day, her oldest son, Patrick, solemnly asked her, 'Will Dad know we've moved here?'

She coldly replied, 'No, he will never know. That's the whole point.'

Of course the main reason for the move was to get cheaper rent. However, Patrick never forgave her. It seemed so unjust how he blamed her when it was their father who had deserted them.

Owen and Nancy helped her a lot with money in those years. She was their big sister who knew everything as far as they were concerned and they were protective towards her.

Patrick and John, the second-oldest boy, took up work on boats, becoming officers, and even captains, on big coastal vessels. As far as they were aware, their father had come out of the sea and they felt the call of the sea too. The youngest boy, Conan, had been too young to even remember his father but suddenly, when a teenager, he plunged, inexplicably, into grief over his father who had never returned from sea. Micky was flabbergasted at how much he suddenly missed a father he would not have remembered at all, seeing he was a baby when his father had left for war. She assumed that he had been influenced by Patrick, who had at least some memories of their father and felt superior to the others as a result.

Bernie never returned to Australia, at least as far as she was aware. She had moved far away from her last address, the only address he knew, because Sydney rents were too high. She had angrily given up waiting for him any longer. She thought he probably remarried bigamously in Ireland. As far as she and her family were concerned, it was as if the sea which he had come from had swallowed him up and never spat him out.

(Based on a true story of an Australian woman born before the First World War.)

Anna's Escape From Europe

I was fourteen when Hitler's army invaded my homeland, Hungary. My father had died a few years before. He had been a doctor. Like young people nowadays, I wasn't interested in politics or my father's stories of the First World War. I and my schoolfriends giggled together and were in intense rivalry to get the best marks at school. I wanted to be a doctor. Jewish people in Budapest in those times were regarded as intellectual and witty before the anti-Semitic German occupation. Once, when I was a young girl, I was crossing the bridge over the beautiful river that flows through Budapest when I saw a group of Hitler youth terrorising a well dressed Jewish man. I felt sickened and hurried home.

Budapest was an elegant city with a vibrant intellectual culture and interesting nightlife, making it fun to be young, but the German occupation ended that. We invented crazy dances and fashions, like young people do nowadays, to rebel against our parents, and we smoked too. Nowadays, young people abuse illegal drugs, which are a source of misery and crime. I used to fear the Hitler Youth. Nowadays in Australia, I fear drug-related crime and radical young men who tell me to go back to where I came from. I think the far right are only a noisy minority in Australia, though.

One day, we heard along the grapevine, as you say in Australia, that the Russian army was advancing. We heard the Russians were seeking vengeance and saw everyone as Nazis even if we hated the German invaders. Russian soldiers raped and plundered wherever they went. My mother bought me a ticket on the black market to get a coach to Berlin. I had an aunt there. My mother sent me alone to the pick-up point, telling me that she would come later. She sternly ordered me that I must get on that bus, whatever happened, even if she hadn't got there in time.

I got on the coach at the very last minute with a cold, sinking feeling. I realised my mother could only afford to buy one ticket and that she gave it to me to save me. I wondered if I would ever see her again.

Years after the war, I and John went back to Hungary to visit my mother. I was eager to meet with my old schoolfriends. My mother told me most of them had died. Some of them had committed suicide after being gang-raped by Russian soldiers, while others had been killed. My mother told me how Russian soldiers had gone from door to door looking for young women and even little girls. They kept asking her, 'Where is your daughter?' The Russian soldiers had turned the house upside down looking for me.

On my arrival home on that visit, my mother had proudly rushed up to me with a china doll that I had always hated. I felt so angry that out of all my old treasures my mother had saved that simpering doll. However, I swallowed my anger and managed to graciously accept the doll in its faded costume and I embraced my mother who was now so tiny and frail.

During the war years, when I joined my aunt in Berlin, we went very hungry. The British and Americans began to drop bombs every night. The bombers flew under the cover of darkness. It was very heartening to think that before long Hitler's rule of terror would be crushed and so we steeled our nerves to the bombing. There were piles of rubble everywhere and the acrid reek of dust. There was a lot of looting going on for goods to trade or sell on the black market. The bombing left many people homeless. I startled some youths at night in the moonlight in a woodland. They looked so ghostly with moonlight shining off their skin and fair hair. I had gone out, defying the curfew, to see the moon over the trees. It seemed so silly in wartime to want to see moonlight.

One day I developed excruciating abdominal pain and went to hospital. All I remember was waking up amidst piles of rubble with dust rising up and stinging my nose and throat. I was half lying on the lap of a young nurse named Rita who had her arms protectively around me. I just told her, 'I want to die at home.' Rita helped me through the rubble and out of the hospital. I somehow made my way to my aunt's place.

After a few months, young people were called up to help the German war effort. I had vowed never to go back to hospital as I feared the hospital would be bombed again. To this day, I'm very anxious in modern Australian hospitals because of the memory of the bombing during the war. However, as I would be exempted from joining the German war effort if I were hospitalised, I stifled my fear and returned. Rita almost fainted when she saw me as she was sure I had died. I probably should have died as the surgery had been incomplete and the incision not stitched up. The surgeon reopened the wound and removed infected tissue. The incision was stitched up this time but I was left unable to bear children.

Unbelievably, I awoke in hospital, for the second time, surrounded by rubble. Rita was holding me in her arms again. She told me that God must have a purpose for me as he had saved my life twice when the hospital was bombed. I told her she was lucky too, as she had also survived two bombings. I don't know what became of Rita.

After I came to Australia, I met some Australians who would coldly tell me I should only feel gratitude after coming to Australia to resettle after the war. I am eternally grateful the allies succeeded in crushing the Third Reich but I am human and I can't help but remember my wartime experiences of suffering. It can be very hard to fit in at times when Australians around me have lived safe, contented, abundant lives and aren't haunted by flashbacks to war in Europe. Even nice people often don't understand it.

I had always remembered my mother's instructions to get to where the British forces were once the British, Americans and Russians began to advance, like a three-pronged pincer, on Berlin. I had been astonished when my mother had given me all of our jewellery before I left to board the coach to Berlin. My aunt and I bartered our jewellery for food that a British soldier got for us off the black market, or so he said. It was probably purloined from British army stores. Australians have said he short-changed us and that the British, everywhere they went, politely took the best and sent it to England. However, that's the way the world was in colonial times. The British, the Germans the Belgians and the Dutch all had empires then. That English soldier was as thin and poor as I was at the time and I was a refugee. He had a sweet, rather childish face. His parents had brought him up well to have manners and show respect,which is so unlike nowadays when some youth don't even stand up for old people on the bus or train. He had never seen jewellery and gold watches like those we traded with him. He said he was going to give a ring to his sweetheart and a diamond pendant to his mother. I liked him. I hope he had a good life after the war.

I met John Moharos in a refugee camp. He was a blond Hungarian while I'm dark from when the Mongols occupied Hungary. I have old photographs from that time. John looked like the Duke of Edinburgh in his prime. He thought I looked like Greta Garbo. I had skin that tanned well. I had long, glamorous brown hair styled like the film stars. I had slanted, very dark eyes from our Mongolian heritage. Everyone was slim after the war. Of course now I am old. I had my hair cropped short as soon as I arrived in Australia and John was so disappointed.

We were offered resettlement in Canada or Australia. Canada would have been much easier for us because the climate was what we were used to with four definite seasons while in Australia the seasons flow into each other. However, I chose Australia because it was as far away from Europe as I could be and so there would be the least risk of invasion. People have asked me if I have forgiven our German enemies and I can only say I hated them with all my heart for what they did to Hungary and Europe. It's easy for the modern people in Australia to preach forgiveness when they have never been through war.

I remember John and me arriving in Australia at Christmas time. There was much confusion after the war when resources were stretched very thin and there had to be hasty, rough and ready solutions in those desperate times. Our first summer was in scorching summer conditions in a hut with sheets of iron for a roof. It was like living in an oven. The sun was intense and glaring. The heat seemed to bounce off the roof and earth and the wilted, yellow grass. Stunted gum trees provided no shade. We were used to white Christmases with dazzling, pure white snow everywhere and covering the fir trees. A kind church group invited us all to Christmas dinner in a church hall. The traditional Christmas roast dinner was too heavy for summer. Cold meats and salad would have been better. The food was delicious but plain compared with traditional Hungarian food, where there are all kinds of stuffed dumplings and pastries. I ate roast lamb for the first time. I felt sorry for the lambs which are so sweet and innocent, but this is part of life in Australia. I ate my first slice of delicious pavlova on my first Christmas in Australia. The small decorated pine branch, already turning brown, in a corner looked pathetic when I thought of the snow-covered trees in Hungary at Christmas time but I felt full of hope for my new life. We were just grateful to have escaped war-torn Europe.

John had trained before the war in engineering and architectural drafting and drawing. He got work in Sydney but he was more skilled than his Australian counterparts, which made some of them very jealous. A fellow worker sabotaged a beautiful architectural drawing John was working on by deliberately spilling ink over it. John wasn't going to start the drawing all over again and walked out. He got work as a chauffeur for members of parliament and diplomats. He got a lot of offers from ASIO and the media to give them information on anything they discussed or about any scandals, such as them being driven to homes of their mistresses or boyfriends, but John refused. The people he chauffeured were democratic, well educated people and they treated him with respect, whatever their politics or private lives were, and John wasn't going to betray them.

I returned to Germany and Hungary many decades after the war and the cities had been rebuilt. However, they were now very unfamiliar. I was glad to return to Australia, who took us in after the war. I still feel safer in Australia than anywhere else.

(A true story as told to me by Anna herself. Her name has been changed.)